P9-DDB-988
FRIENDS
OF ACPL
3 1833 00694 0677

Read-to-Me
Storybook

Read-to-Me
Storybook

Compiled by the Child Study Association of America

Illustrated by
LOIS LENSKI

Thomas Y. Crowell Company
NEW YORK

THIRD PRINTING MAY 1948

Manufactured in the United States of America

Acknowledgments

For the privilege of reprinting the following copyrighted poems and stories, grateful acknowledgment and thanks are extended to the publishers indicated:

Unknown, "Wee Robin's Christmas Day" from *Scottish Fairy and Folk Tales,* collected by Sir George Douglas, by permission of Charles Scribner's Sons, publisher.

Dorothy W. Baruch, *Pitter Patter,* by permission of William R. Scott, Inc., publisher.

Elsa Beskow, *The Tale of the Wee Little Old Woman,* translated from the Swedish by Marion Woodburn, by permission of Harper and Brothers, publisher.

Margaret Wise Brown, "The Terrrrible Tigerrr" from *Another Here and Now Story Book,* edited by Lucy Sprague Mitchell, published and copyright 1937 by E. P. Dutton & Co., Inc., New York; "The Wonderful Day" from *The Fish with the Deep Sea Smile* by Margaret Wise Brown, published and copyright 1938 by E. P. Dutton & Co., Inc., New York.

Charims, *Surprise,* copyright 1935 by Whitman Publishing Co., reprinted by permission of the publisher.

Mary Mapes Dodge, "Snow-Flakes" from *St. Nicholas Magazine,* by permission of D. Appleton-Century Company, Inc., publisher.

Eugene Field, "Why Do the Bells of Christmas Ring?", reprinted from *Sharps and Flats,* copyright 1900, 1901, 1928 by Julia Sutherland Field, used by permission of the publishers, Charles Scribner's Sons.

Rachel Field, "I'd Like to Be a Lighthouse" from *Taxis and Toadstools,* copyright 1926 by Doubleday & Company, Inc.

Marjorie Flack, *Christopher,* copyright 1935 by Charles Scribner's Sons, used by permission of the publishers, Charles Scribner's Sons.

Katharine T. Garbutt, *Michael the Colt,* by permission of Houghton Mifflin Company, publisher.

Marion Florence Lansing, "Seeing the World" from *Quaint Old Stories*, by permission of Ginn and Company, publisher.

Winifred Milius, *Here Comes Daddy*, reprinted by permission of William R. Scott, Inc., publisher.

Lucy Sprague Mitchell, "How Spot Found a Home" from *Here and Now Story Book*, published and copyright 1921 by E. P. Dutton & Co., Inc., New York; "Lots of Places to Sit" and "New Clothes" from *Another Here and Now Story Book*, published and copyright 1937 by E. P. Dutton & Co., Inc., New York.

Estelle McInnes Upson, *Sneezer*, copyright 1945 by Whitman Publishing Co., reprinted by permission of the publisher.

Rhea Wells, "Peppi and the Custard" from *Peppi the Duck*, copyright 1927 by Doubleday & Company, Inc.

Preface

This *Read-to-Me Storybook* for children two to four years of age is a pioneering venture. It offers parents and nursery-school teachers and others who live with the very youngest a balanced assortment of stories and verse, some of them fanciful, some of them funny, and some about the familiar everyday happenings wherein young listeners may recognize themselves.

Before children are ready for school and long before they can possibly read well enough to enjoy reading for themselves, stories and verse become a necessary part of life for them. Even before a child can understand the words, the patter and snatches of song or nonsense rhymes that are told or read to him become part of a shared experience with his parents. When stories and verse are put down on paper, they take more definite and more lasting form. There they are, to be read and re-read to each member of the family, furnishing treasured memories and sentiments which bind older and younger together with subtle but strong bonds.

Reading to a child does much more than amuse him or send him quietly off to sleep. The stories and the rhythms sink in; the people and creatures become part of the child's life; words take on meaning as images and symbols. Furthermore, reading to a child conveys the mood of the reader as well as the intent of the author. In the very tones of his parent's voice the child learns that a piece has been familiar to the reader from his own childhood, or that he feels the enthusiasm of a new discovery. Even after the child can read for himself, reading aloud to him will go far to keep a vital relationship alive.

Today, no family can continue to live entirely on its own "inheritance" of good literature from the past. Those who live with youngsters need to know the new creations constantly being made available, as well as their own almost personal childhood favorites. The child needs modern stories to keep him close to his contemporaries; the adult needs them, too, to help him understand the new generation. Finding what is suitable among the new, however, is not always easy for the individual parent or teacher; and selecting among all that is offered takes time, training, and perhaps special talent. This book is therefore designed to meet a real need.

Ten of the stories in this book were especially written for it by authors who have already endeared themselves to children. Others are reprinted here from varied sources because they seem to be permanent parts of the child's world. A few have appeared separately as whole picture books. The verses, traditional as well as modern, represent the timelessness of childhood's interests.

The book was planned by the Children's Book Committee of the Child Study Association of America, consisting of parents, librarians, and writers, under the chairmanship of Mrs. Hugh Grant Straus. The stories and verses were lovingly selected by members of the committee under the direction of Josette Frank.

We hope that the book will be widely useful since the committee in its selections has provided for many different moods and occasions.

SIDONIE MATSNER GRUENBERG, *Director*
Child Study Association of America

Contents

Read-to-Me
Storybook

THE WONDERFUL DAY

Margaret Wise Brown

"Whee," said the kittens, "what a wonderful day! Whee what a wonderful day!" and they arched their backs and spread their paws and sharpened their claws on the rug.

"Woof," said the big dog, "I'm glad I'm awake —Woof what a wonderful day!" And he stretched and yawned and his black eyes were shiny as he woke in the wonderful day.

And all the little birds in the trees whistled and chirped—"The day is young, we are young, the year is young, Spring Spring Spring is young, Spring is green. Cheer Cheer Cheer Spring is here!"

But the little boy didn't wake up.

LOIS
LENSKI

The sun shone in through the window warm and cool. It made the white in the room shiny. A soft breeze blew in the window and ruffled the curls on the little boy's head.

But the little boy didn't wake up.

The birds fluttered their wings outside and the sunlight burned green on the trees.

But the little boy didn't wake up.

The kittens climbed on the little boy's back and blinked their starry eyes.

The old dog sat by the little boy's bed and stared at him right in the face. "I will look him awake," said the old dog, "for he must see this beautiful day."

But the little boy didn't wake up.

Trapper Trapper Trapper chattered the gray squirrel, and his claws went scratching over the roof.

Tack Tack Tack Tack pecked the woodpecker in the old wooden tree.

And a clear note like falling water came from the throat of a bird.

Then the little boy woke up.

LOTS OF PLACES TO SIT

Lucy Sprague Mitchell

Mollie has lots of places to sit in her house. Sometimes she just sits on the floor. That's when she plays with her blocks. She doesn't even sit on the rug. She spills the blocks out of their box, and she makes them all go in nice long rows. Sometimes she puts little, tiny, colored blocks on top. That's to make it pretty. Sometimes she does sit on the rug. That's when she has Little Ann with her. Little Ann is her doll. Little Ann likes to go to sleep on the rug. So Mollie makes a bed for her out of two blocks and puts Little Ann to sleep on them.

Mollie doesn't always sit on the floor. Oh, no! For Mollie has a chair that is all her own. She can back into it and bend her knees, and there she is! It just fits her. Father couldn't sit in Mollie's chair; Mother couldn't sit in Mollie's chair; Benny couldn't sit in Mollie's chair. Just Mollie! Sometimes Mollie sits with Little Ann in her lap. Little

Ann likes to sit in Mollie's lap in her chair. She told Mollie so. Father and Mother and Benny didn't hear her. Just Mollie! When Mollie has supper, she sits all alone in her chair, and Little Ann sits all alone on a pillow beside her!

Mollie doesn't always sit on the floor or in her chair. Sometimes Father comes in. That's when she has finished her supper. "Ready for a story, Mollie?" he says. And Mollie says, "Yes, Father, tell me a story!" And where do you think Mollie sits when Father tells her a story? She doesn't sit on the floor. Oh, no! She doesn't sit in her chair. Oh, no! She sits in a place she likes better than the floor and better, even, than her chair. She sits in Father's lap! And sometimes Little Ann sits in Mollie's lap at the same time. Little Ann sits in Mollie's lap; Mollie sits in Father's lap; and Father sits in a chair. And they all have a story together. Then Mollie goes to bed.

Yes, Mollie has lots of places to sit in her house.

THE LIGHTS IN GEORGIE'S HOUSE

Kathleen Bernath

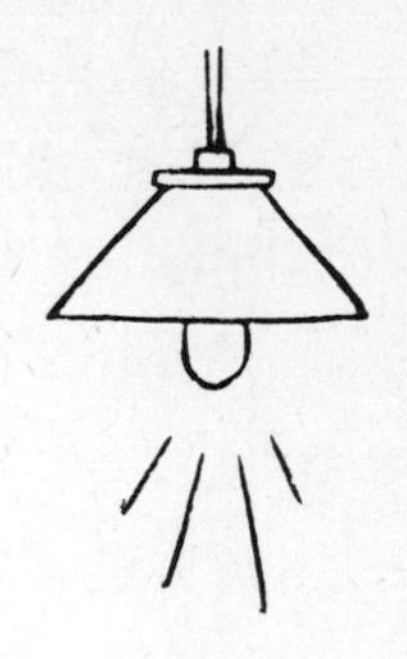

Every room
in Georgie's house
has a button
you can press.

When you press—
wait—can you guess
What happens
when you press?

That's right—
on goes the light!

Stand on tiptoe,
reach up high,
Push and press
with all your might—

Turn on the light!

SURPRISE

Charims

Molly told Mops she was going to have a birthday in three more days.

So she sat down at her table and wrote invitations to her five little playmates.

Then Molly and Mops mailed the invitations.

One day passed, two days passed, three days passed. On the fourth day Molly woke up early . . . it was her birthday.

She looked everywhere for Mops but Mops could not be found.

Molly called and called but Mops did not come.

"How can I have a party without Mops?" thought Molly.

Molly put on her party dress and waited for her guests.

The five little guests arrived.

Molly started to open her presents.

Just as she was opening the last present Mops came dashing in.

Mops led Molly and her guests across the lawn to the dog house in back of the barn . . . then Mops barked and barked for Molly to open the door.

And there was Mops' present to Molly.

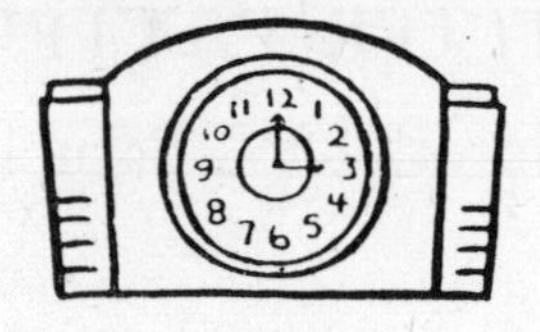

THE CLOCK

Tick, tock, tick, tock,
Merrily sings the clock;
It's time for work,
It's time for play,
So it sings throughout the day.
Tick, tock, tick, tock,
Merrily sings the clock.

PITTER PATTER

Dorothy W. Baruch

One day it rained and it rained. Pitter patter, it rained in the town. Pitter patter, it rained in the country.

Pitter patter, pitter patter.
It rained on a truck that went
rumbling through town.
Rumbledy rumble, rumbledy rumble.

It rained and it rained
And the truck got all wet.

Way up in the sky over the town
flew an airplane.
Brrrum flew the plane in the sky.
Brrum, brrum-ummmm.

It rained on the plane *pitter patter.*
It rained and it rained.
And the plane got all wet.

Pitter patter, pitter patter.
Down came the rain on a field in the country.
Moo, said the cow who lived in the field.
Moo—moo—moooo.

It rained on the cow.
It rained and it rained.
And the cow got all wet.

Quack, quack, said the duck as it rained on his back.
Quack, quack, said the duck on his way to the lake.

It rained on the duck *pitter pat, pitter pat.*
And the duck got all wet.

Pitter patter, it rained on a boat on the lake.
Flap, flap went the sail of the boat in the wind.
And the sail and the boat got all wet.

Along came a train, *puff chuff, puff chuff.*
The train blew its whistle, *whoo, whoo whoo!*

Pitter patter went the rain down onto the train.
And the train got all wet.

Along the road came a car, *slippery slish.*
Pitter patter, pitter pat, it rained on the car.
It rained on the top and the hood;
on the back fenders and the front fenders
and the windshield.

It rained and it rained
And the car got all wet.

LOIS
LENSKI

Then down the road came a boy.
He had on galoshes. He wore a raincoat.
He wore a rain hat. And he carried an umbrella.
Splash, *splash*, he walked through the puddles.
Slosh, *slosh*, he walked in the rain.

The boy's galoshes got all wet.
His raincoat got all wet.
His rain hat got all wet.
His umbrella got all wet.

But did the boy get all wet?

No, he didn't. He stayed DRY.

MRS. GOOSE'S RUBBERS

Miriam Clark Potter

One day Mrs. Goose could not find her rubbers. She looked in the same old place in the dark hall closet, and she looked under the bed, and she looked on the back porch; but she could not see them. So she went to Mrs. Pig's house and knocked at the door. When Mrs. Pig came to see who was knocking, Mrs. Goose said: "Have you seen my rubbers?"

"Of course I haven't seen your rubbers, Mrs. Goose," Mrs. Pig told her. "They wouldn't be over here at my house, would they?"

"I don't know," said Mrs. Goose. "I just thought they might be."

Then she went to Mrs. Squirrel's house and knocked at the door. When Mrs. Squirrel came to let her in, Mrs. Goose said, "I just came to see if you had seen my rubbers."

Mrs. Squirrel was making a nut-patty pudding. "No, indeed, I haven't seen your rubbers," she said. "Did you think they were *here?*"

"I didn't know," sighed Mrs. Goose. "I just thought they might be."

Then Mrs. Goose went home. She looked under the stove, she looked behind the door, she looked up on the clock shelf, she looked in the waste paper basket, she looked in the ice-box, but she could not find her rubbers.

Just then Mrs. Sheep went by.

"Oh, Mrs. Sheep," called Mrs. Goose; "have you seen my rubbers?"

Mrs. Sheep stopped by the fence. "Why, no, I haven't seen your rubbers," she said. "Where do you usually keep them?"

"In their same old place in the dark hall closet," said Mrs. Goose. "But they are not there."

Mrs. Sheep thought for a minute, and then she said, "Why do you want your rubbers, anyway, Mrs. Goose? The sun is shining."

"Well, it might rain tomorrow," Mrs. Goose replied, "and then I'd want them."

"That's right," said Mrs. Sheep. "Come to think of it, I don't know where *my* rubbers are, either. I'd better go home and look them up." And she hurried on.

Still Mrs. Goose could *not* find her rubbers. She looked in the teakettle, she looked on the back stairs, she looked in the bread box, she looked under her pillow, and then she got a ladder and climbed up on the roof and stared all around; but her black eyes did not spy them anywhere.

"Dear me, dear me," she sighed, "where can my rubbers *be?*"

Then she ate her supper and went to bed. Next morning when she woke up, rain was coming down —*drip, drip, drip*, on the roof. "Oh, it *is* raining today," said Mrs. Goose, "and I've got to go to market, and I haven't found my rubbers, and I'll get my poor feet all wet!"

She got up and made her bed and ate her breakfast. She dusted her house; and then she just *had* to go to market. The rain was coming down in big bursts and splashes and there were puddles all over the sidewalk.

"I *must* find my rubbers!" thought Mrs. Goose. And she looked and looked in all the same places, but they did not turn up. "Well," she sighed, "I shall have to go without them. That's *what!*" And she put on her coat and bonnet, took her big green umbrella from its place in the dark hall closet, and started out. She shut the door behind her, locked it with the tiny key, and stepped out on her porch. Then she put her big green umbrella up.

"Plop! Plop!" Two big somethings hit her on the head and almost knocked her bonnet off. They fell down on the porch behind her. "What can they be?" thought Mrs. Goose. She turned around and looked at them. They were her rubbers!

"I must have put them inside my umbrella," said Mrs. Goose. "Oh, now I remember! I put them there so they would not be lost. But it would have been a good deal better if I had put them back in their same place, in the dark hall closet."

Then she put her rubbers on, and went splashing along through the puddles on her way to market.

THE WIND

Lois Lenski

Hugh,
Hugh,
What did you do?
Open the door and
Let the wind blow through?
Shoosh—whew!
How the wind blew!
It blew the table right out of the door,
It blew the chairs right off of the floor,
It blew everything out and then blew some more,
Shoosh—whew!
Hugh,
Hugh,
Where are you?
Did you blow out too
When the wind blew through?
Shoosh—whew!

TWO FARMERS

Margaret Wise Brown

There was a great big farmer
And a very little farmer.

They had farms side by side
Only the big farmer's farm was very big
And the little farmer's farm was so very little
No one could see it but the little farmer.

He had very little cows
And very little pigs
And tiny tiny chickens
And very little hills
And very little vegetables
And a little tiny barn
THAT LITTLE FARMER!

Not so the big farmer
Everything was big.
Big cows
Big pigs
Big roosters
Big hills
Big vegetables
And a great big hulk of a barn.
THAT GREAT BIG FARMER!

LOIS
LENSKI

Early in the morning his cows
Made a great big noise
  Moooooooooooo.
And just as the sun rose
His great big roosters began to crow
  CCKADOODLEDOO.
And the sound went up in the air over his great big
    hills
And woke up all the big pigs
With a loud GRUNT GRUNT
And a SNUFFLE, WUFFLE WOOP

And woke up the big farmer with a great big yawn
And sent him out into the dawn
With a great big bucket to get some milk
From his great big cows.

And the noise woke up the little farmer
Next door on his little farm
And he got up with a little yawn
And went out into the dawn
With a little bucket to milk his little cows.
THAT LITTLE FARMER!

Then he fed his little chickens
And he fed his little pigs
And he picked some little vegetables
And
He fed his little self
Fried potatoes
And Milk
And Bacon
And A LITTLE TINY SOFT BOILED EGG.

And the big farmer
Ate a GREAT BIG BREAKFAST and a GREAT BIG SOFT BOILED EGG

With a great big napkin
Tucked under his chin.

Then after breakfast he went out
And oiled his GREAT BIG FARM TRUCK
So it would go easily and would not squeak.

Then he took his great big oil can and oiled his
GREAT BIG TRACTOR
Then he oiled his
GREAT BIG HAY RICK

And he gave his GREAT BIG HORSE
A great big drink and harnessed him up
To his great big hay rick and off he went
To a great big field where he raked yellow hay
Into a GREAT BIG HAY STACK.
Big birds flew overhead.

And the little farmer gave his LITTLE HORSE
A little drink and harnessed him to his little hay rick
And off he went to his little field where he raked
the yellow hay
Into a LITTLE HAYSTACK.
Little birds flew overhead.

Then the big farmer pulled his big farmer's hat
Down over his nose and lay down on his big haystack
And took a nap.

And the little farmer pulled his little farmer's hat
Down over his nose and lay down in his little
    haystack
And took a nap.

And the sun shone on them.
And warm winds blew about them
And the bees buzzed
And the flowers grew
And when they woke up it was afternoon.

SNEEZER

Estelle McInnes Upson

The children loved the little train. Every morning he came chug-chugging up the hill. They could hear the little train long before he came in sight of the quiet little country town.

Other trains went choo-choo-chooing along but not this train. He would make the funniest sounds . . . ah-CHOO-ah-CHOO—ah-CHOOOO as he rolled merrily along the countryside. That was why the children named him "SNEEZER."

Sneezer loved the green hills and the friendly horses and cows in the fields. He liked to watch his old friend the river as it went rushing by, hurrying, hurrying down to the sea.

And Sneezer loved the gardens and the white houses he passed every day.

"HURRAY! Just like a snake!" Sneezer cried as he rushed around the curves. First this way then that way, he would go. "WHEEEEE! This is fun! This is fun!" Sneezer exclaimed as he dashed lickety-split down the hills.

"GET UP STEAM! GET UP STEAM!" chugged little Sneezer as he puffed and puffed his way to the very TOP of the hill.

"Hellooooooo!" called Sneezer to all the children. Some of the children sat on the fence and waved as he went by. Some of the children waved to him from the windows of their little white houses. And some of the children even ran down the track after Sneezer. They called, "Wait!" But Sneezer only said, "Ah-

CHOO-ah-CHOO!" The children could not catch him because he was too fast for them.

Soon he would disappear into the dark entrance of a tunnel in the side of the mountain—just like a rabbit disappearing into a hole in the ground!

The engineer and the fireman loved Sneezer for he was the most well-behaved little train in all the land. He was always on time and always happy. Not only that . . . Sneezer was the cleanest, shiniest train anyone had ever seen! Yes, sir! Sneezer was the jolliest, nicest little train that EVER was!

One day Sneezer was going happily along as he did every day. He had gone up and down a hill and past the little white houses, when something very unusual happened. He came to a high bridge and stopped—suddenly! The stop was so sudden that some of the passengers were thrown out of their seats and into the aisle.

The engineer was VERY much surprised. This was not at all like Sneezer.

What ever could the trouble be?

The engineer coaxed and pleaded but Sneezer

would not budge. He would just snort a few times, then stand there quietly. Suddenly, someone shouted, "Look! The bridge! The bridge! It's falling!" Sure enough, while everyone watched, the bridge fell into the deep river.

Then the engineer and the fireman and the passengers knew why Sneezer had been so stubborn. If he had not stopped they would have fallen into the water.

Everyone was very happy and grateful to Sneezer. He had saved their lives! That day, all the people in the town came to see their hero. A band played music while the mayor of the town presented Sneezer with a shiny new medal. Everyone clapped and waved flags while the band played. All the children decorated Sneezer with flags and streamers. "Three cheers for Sneezer!" shouted the children. "Hurrah for Sneezer!" Sneezer was very proud and very happy. Then away went Sneezer with all the streamers flying in the breeze. The people waved to their hero until he was out of sight.

SUSAN BLUE

Kate Greenaway

Oh, Susan Blue,
How do you do?
Please may I go for a walk with you?
Where shall we go?
Oh, I know—
Down in the meadow where the cow-
slips grow!

THE TALE OF THE WEE LITTLE OLD WOMAN

Elsa Beskow

Translated from the Swedish by Marion Woodburn

There once was a wee little old woman
  Who had a wee little house
And a wee little table and a wee little chair
  And a wee little stool and a wee little milkpail;

And a wee little cat that said; "meow,"

And a wee little cow that said; "moo-o-o."

One day the wee little old woman took her little
    wee stool
  And went out to milk her little wee cow.

She put the wee bit of milk on the little wee table.

Just then the little wee cat came in—

First he jumped up on the little wee stool,
Then on the little wee chair and then on the
little wee table, and drank up all the milk!—

But then the wee little old woman came back—

SCAT, CAT!!!!

And the cat ran away to the woods and NEVER
came back again.

MUDDY MOUSE

Helen and Alf Evers

Every day the Mouse family went for a walk.
When they came to a mud puddle,
Father Mouse walked around it.
Mother Mouse walked around it.
Sister Mouse and Brother Mouse walked around it, too.
But little Muddy Mouse walked right through it.
He liked mud.
His friend, the horse, didn't like mud.
The cow didn't like mud.
The dog and the cat didn't like mud.
But Muddy Mouse liked mud so much
that he cried when there wasn't any.
One day Muddy Mouse played on the muddy pasture road.

He rolled over and over down the road.
Muddy Mouse thought it was fun, because the road was full of sticky brown mud.
But the mud stuck to his fur!
More and more mud stuck to Muddy Mouse, until he looked like a big brown ball of mud.
The tip of his tail stuck out of one side of the ball, and the tip of his nose stuck out of the other.
There was so much mud on Muddy Mouse that he couldn't walk.
He couldn't talk,
he couldn't even cry, and he wanted to cry very much.
Just then the black cat and her two kittens came along.
They thought Muddy Mouse was a big brown ball, so they started to play with him.

They rolled him back and forth.
They rolled him around and around
until Muddy Mouse was dizzy.
Then the black cat and her two kittens gave Muddy Mouse a push,
and away he rolled over the pasture.
He didn't stop until he reached the fence.
After the black cat and her two kittens had scampered away,
Father Mouse and Mother Mouse came out to look for Muddy Mouse.
They looked under every stone and behind every bush.
But they would never have found Muddy Mouse at all,
if he hadn't wiggled the tip of his tail, to call for help.
Then Father Mouse and Mother Mouse scraped and scraped,
and scrubbed and scrubbed at the big brown ball of mud.
At last they saw an ear, then a bright little eye, then a smooth gray back.
And, after a long long time, there stood Muddy Mouse—all of him.
He danced and squeaked with happiness,
because he didn't have a single bit of mud on him.

Every day after that, the Mouse family still went for a walk.

And when they came to a mud puddle, Father Mouse still walked around it.

Mother Mouse walked around it.

Sister Mouse and Brother Mouse walked around the puddle, too.

But Muddy Mouse didn't walk around it.

He RAN around it.

HERE COMES DADDY

Winifred Milius

A boy named Peter had a cat named Finnigan.

One day just before supper Peter and Finnigan went out to the corner to watch for Peter's Daddy to come home. They looked up and down the street. They saw a lady with a baby carriage, a man sweeping leaves, two boys on a bicycle, and a little spotted dog. But no Daddy yet.

Pretty soon along came someone pushing a little wagon in front of him. Could this be Daddy coming home?

No. It was a delivery boy. He stopped and took some groceries into a red house and went away.

No Daddy yet.

A little truck came up the street. Could this be Daddy coming home?

No. It was a bread truck. It stopped in front of the grocery store and the man delivered some bread.

No Daddy yet.

Around the corner came a car. A lady and a dog were in it. Could this be Daddy coming home?

No. The car went by without stopping.
"P-s-s-s-s-s-t!" said Finnigan to the dog.

No Daddy yet.

A big coal truck lumbered up the street. Could this be Daddy coming home?

No. The coal truck stopped at a house to deliver some coal.

Clankety, clankety. Out rattled the coal into barrels. Roll it away. Put it in the celler.

No Daddy yet.

A great big moving van drove up and stopped. Could this be Daddy coming home?

No. Men got out and carried tables and chairs and lamps and a big couch into a house.

No Daddy yet.

Up the street came a truck squirting water from its sides. Could this be Daddy coming home?

No. It was a street sprinkling truck and water swish-sh-sh-sh-shed all over the street.

No Daddy yet.

Clop-clop, clop-clop came a horse and wagon.
Jingle, jangle went the bells on the wagon.
Could this be Daddy coming home?

No. It was the junk man carting off some scrap.
He waved to Peter and Finnigan as he went by.

No Daddy yet.

Then around the corner came a bus all full of people. Could this be Daddy coming home?

The bus stopped and out got a little old man with an umbrella, a tall thin lady, a boy with a suitcase, and a man carrying a newspaper. "Here's Daddy, now!" shouted Peter.

Then Daddy took Peter's hand and they all walked home together.

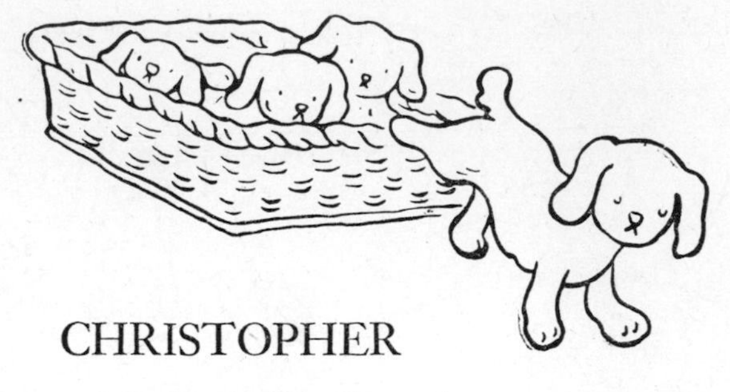

CHRISTOPHER

Marjorie Flack

Once upon a time there were four very small puppies who lived in a basket with their mother.

Now one of these puppies was much larger and much stronger than any of the other puppies.

He was so much larger and so much stronger than the others that while they could only crawl around on their tummies, he could stand up on his four fat little legs.

One day this large strong puppy put his front paws up over the side of the basket and he wiggled and wiggled, until, flop, there he was outside the basket! Then off he wobbled to see what he could find. His mother had to carry him back.

So he was named Christopher, for Christopher Columbus, because he was such a brave explorer.

When Christopher grew larger he did not live in the basket with his mother any more. He lived in a house with a little girl named Sally and a boy named

Tom. The larger Christopher grew the more he liked exploring.

Christopher liked to explore the mole hills and around trees, and under the kitchen porch and in the brook and many other places to see what he could find.

But most of all he liked to go exploring with Sally and Tom in the car.

Sometimes they would stop at the grocery shop and Christopher would find a cat to tease.

Sometimes they would stop at the butcher shop and Christopher would find a bone. Sometimes, best of all, they would stop at Grandmother's house and they would all find cookies there.

One Sunday morning when Christopher was out exploring the garden he heard Sally calling,

"Here, Christopher. Here, Christopher!" And he heard Tom calling,

"Here, Christopher. Come here, Christopher!"

So Christopher ran into the house to see why they wanted him.

"We are going in the car to Grandmother's house this afternoon," said Tom.

When Christopher heard the word "car" he wagged his tail and barked with joy.

"And we are going to give you a nice bath now so you will be all beautiful and clean when you go with us," said Sally.

When Christopher heard the word "bath" he stopped wagging his tail and he stopped barking for joy; and he ran up stairs and he hid under the bed. Christopher hid under the bed because he did not like baths.

But Sally pulled him out and then she held him in the tub while Tom scrubbed him. Then Tom held him while Sally scrubbed him and then they rinsed Christopher. They rinsed him in bluing water until he was as white as snow. Then they rubbed him and tied him up in a towel and put him in the sun in the kitchen to dry.

"Now," said Sally, "you are a beautiful clean Christopher!"

"Lie down," said Tom, "and stay there until you are nice and dry."

Then Sally and Tom went away and Christopher was left alone in the sun in the kitchen to dry.

But Christopher did not stay there. He saw a squirrel outside the window, so he pushed open the screen door. Out he ran, towel and all.

But up the squirrel ran, up high in the tree. So

Christopher went exploring under the porch and around the trees and in the brook and in the mole hills until he was no longer white as snow.

Then Christopher saw a rabbit looking at him, looking at him from under a bush. Quickly Christopher dashed over the ground—quickly he scrambled under the bush, but—he stopped. Christopher stopped because he was caught by the towel in the bush!

Christopher tried to run back but he could not go back. He tried to go this way and he tried to go that way. The more he tried to get away the more Christopher got tangled up in the bush. There was nothing for him to do but wait.

Christopher saw the squirrel jumping from tree to tree.

He saw the rabbit come hopping about.

He saw a field mouse come running out.

But poor Christopher could not chase them, he could not move, he could only wait. He waited and waited until at last he heard Sally calling,

"Here, Christopher. Here, Christopher!"

And he heard Tom calling,

"Here, Christopher. Come here, Christopher!"

But Christopher could not go to them, because he was tangled in the bush.

So he called to them. He called, "YIP—YIPPPPP-YIP."

At last he saw them come running to him, and Sally said,

"Naughty Christopher. You naughty Christopher. Look, you are all muddy and dirty!"

And Tom said, "We'll have to give you a bath all over again."

So Sally and Tom untangled Christopher from the bush and they took him home and they gave him a bath all over again. They scrubbed him and they rinsed him in bluing water and they rubbed him and they wrapped him in another towel and put him in the sun in the kitchen to dry.

"Now," said Tom, "stay there, stay there until you are all nice and dry, so you can go with us in the car to Grandmother's house."

So Sally and Tom went away and soon Christopher saw the squirrel outside the window.

He saw the rabbit looking out from the bush.

He saw the field mouse come running out.

But he stayed there. Christopher stayed right there in the sun in the kitchen to dry. When Tom and Sally were all ready to go, there was Christopher all nice and dry and as clean and as white as snow!

So Christopher and Sally and Tom all rode away in the car to Grandmother's house to see what they could find.

WHAT DOES LITTLE BIRDIE SAY

Alfred Tennyson

What does little birdie say
In her nest at peep of day?
Let me fly, says little birdie,
Mother, let me fly away.
Birdie, rest a little longer,
Till the little wings are stronger.
So she rests a little longer.
Then she flies away.

HOW SPOT FOUND A HOME

Lucy Sprague Mitchell

Once there was a cat. She was a black and white and yellow cat and the boys on the street called her Spot. For she was a poor cat with no home but the street. When she wanted to sleep, she had to hunt for a dark empty cellar. When she wanted to eat, she had to hunt for a garbage can. So poor Spot was very thin and very unhappy. And much of the time she prowled and yowled and howled.

Now one day Spot was prowling along the fence in the alley. She wanted to find a home. She was saying to herself:

"Meow, meow!
I've no place to eat,
I've no place to sleep,
I've only the street!
Meow, meow, meow!"

Then suddenly she smelled something. Sniff! went her pink little nose. Spot knew it was smoke she smelled. The smoke came out of the chimney of a house. "Where there is smoke there is fire," thought Spot, "and where there is fire, it is warm to lie." So she jumped down from the fence and on her little padded feet ran softly to the door. There she saw an empty milk bottle. "Where there are milk bottles, there is milk," thought Spot, "and where there is milk, it is good to drink." So she slipped in through the door.

Inside was a warm, warm kitchen. Spot trotted softly to the front of the stove and there she curled up. She was very happy, so she closed her eyes and began to sing:

"Purrrr, purrrr,
Curling up warm
To a ball of fur,
I close my eyes
And purr and purr.
Purrrr, purrrr,
Purrrr, purrrr."

Bang! went the kitchen door. Spot opened one sleepy eye. In front of her stood a cross, cross woman. The cross, cross woman scowled. She picked up poor Spot and threw her out of the door, screaming:

"Scat, scat!
You old street cat!
Scat, scat!
And never come back!"

With a bound Spot jumped back to the fence.

"Meow, meow!
I've no place to eat,
I've no place to sleep,
I've only the street.
Meow, meow, meow!"

So she trotted along the fence. In a little while sniff! went her little pink nose again. She smelled more smoke. She stopped by a house with two chimneys. The smoke came out of both chimneys! "Where there are two fires there must be room for me," thought Spot. She jumped off the fence and pattered to the door. By the door there were two empty milk bottles. "Where there is so much milk there will be some for me," thought Spot. But the door was shut tight. Spot ran to the window. It was open! In skipped Spot. There was another warm,

warm kitchen and there was another stove. Spot trotted softly to the stove and curled up happy and warm. She closed her eyes and softly sang:

"Purrrr, purrrr,
Curling up warm
To a ball of fur,
I close my eyes
And purr and purr.
Purrrr, purrrr,
Purrrr, purrrr."

"Ssssspt!" hissed something close by. Spot leapt to her feet. "Ssssspt!" she answered back. For there in front of her stood an enormous black cat. His back was humped, his hair stood on end, and his eyes gleamed and his teeth showed white.

"Ssssspt! leave my rug!
Ssssspt! leave my fire
Ssssspt! leave my milk!
Ssssspt! leave my home!"

Spot gave one great jump out of the window and another great jump to the top of the fence. For Spot was little and thin and the great black cat was strong and big. And he didn't want Spot in his home.

Poor Spot trotted along the fence, thinking:

"Meow, meow!
I've no place to eat,

I've no place to sleep,
I've only the street!
Meow, meow, meow!"

In a little while she smelled smoke again. Sniff! went her little pink nose. This time she stopped by a house with three chimneys. The smoke came out of all the chimneys! "Where there are three fires there *must* be room for me," thought Spot. So she jumped off the fence and pattered to the door. By the door were three empty milk bottles! "Where there is so much milk there must be children," thought Spot and then she began to feeel happy. But the door was shut tight. She trotted to the window. The window was shut tight too! Then she saw some stairs. Up the stairs she trotted. There she found another door and in she slipped. She heard a very pleasant sound.

"I crickle, I crackle,
I flicker, I flare,
I jump from nothing right into the air."

There on the hearth burned an open fire with a warm, warm rug in front of it. On the rug was a little table and on the table were two little mugs of milk. Spot curled up on the rug under the table and began to sing:

"Purrrr, purrrr,
Curling up warm
To a ball of fur,

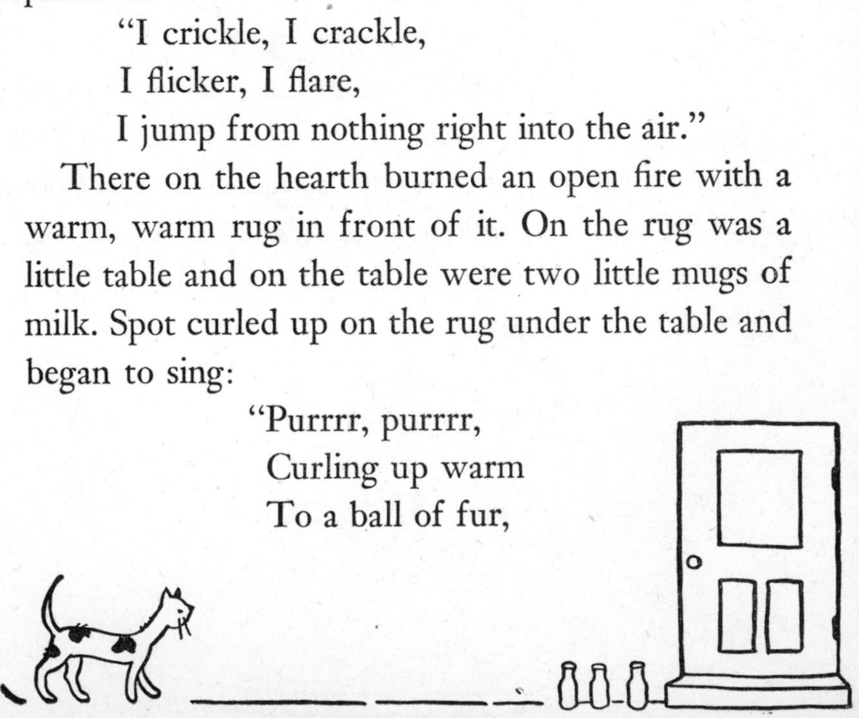

I close my eyes
And purr and purr.
Purrrr, purrrr,
Purrrr, purrrr."

Pat, pat, pat, pat, pat, pat, pat, pat! Spot heard some little feet coming. A little boy in a nightgown ran into the room. "Look," he called, "at the pretty spotted cat under our table!" Then pat, pat, pat, pat, pat! And a little girl in a nightgown ran into the room. "See," she called, "the pussy has come to take supper with us!" Then the little boy, quick as a wink, put a saucer on the floor and poured some of his milk into it and the little girl, quick as a wink, poured some of hers in too.

In and out, in and out, in and out, went Spot's pink tongue lapping up the milk. Then she sat up and washed her face very carefully. Then she curled up and closed her eyes and began to sing. That was her way of saying "Thank you, little boy and little girl! I'm so glad I've found a home!"

"Purrrr, purrrr,
Purrrr, purrrr,
Purrrr, purrrr, purrrr."

WONDERFUL WILLY

Tony Brice

Willy was a little brown dog. He lived with the Smith family.

Mr. Smith was very nice to Willy.

Mrs. Smith was very nice to Willy.

And the Smith boy, Harold, was nicer to Willy than anyone.

So Willy should have been very happy.

But he wasn't happy.

He saw that Mr. Smith didn't walk around on four legs.

He walked on two legs.

So did Mrs. Smith.

And so did Harold Smith.

Willy wanted to walk on just his two hind legs too.

He tried and tried to walk on just his hind legs.

And at last Willy did!

Mr. Smith saw Willy walking on his hind legs.

"How wonderful Willy is!" said Mr. Smith.

"How wonderful Willy is!" said Mrs. Smith

"How VERY wonderful Willy is!" shouted Harold Smith.

The Smiths were very proud of Willy.

They called in their friends and neighbors, to see Willy walking around the living room on his hind legs. It was hard work for Willy to walk around on his hind legs. But he didn't mind, because he was so proud and happy.

One day the Smiths were shopping on Main Street. Willy walked with them, on his hind legs.

Everybody who came along stopped to admire the way Willy walked on two legs. They all thought he was wonderful.

Just then the kind butcher came out of his shop, and put some bones down on the sidewalk for the dogs.

Dogs came running from everywhere. Old dogs, young dogs, black dogs, white dogs, brown dogs, yellow dogs and spotted dogs. Even a little puppy who wasn't old enough to eat a bone, scampered toward the butcher shop.

Willy tried to run on his hind legs. But he couldn't. He could only walk slowly.

He wanted a bone so much that at last he dropped down on all four legs and RAN.

It felt so good to be on four legs again that Willy ran faster than he had ever run before. He ran so fast that he reached the butcher shop first and picked out the biggest, juicest bone of all.

When Willy had eaten his bone and started back to the Smiths, he remembered how proud of him Mr. Smith had been, when he walked on just his hind legs.

Willy remembered how proud Mrs. Smith had been.

He remembered how very proud Harold Smith had been.

Poor Willy thought the Smiths would be ashamed of him because he had stopped walking on two legs and had run on all four.

And right on Main Street in front of all their friends too!

Willy walked very slowly with his tail between his legs. He felt very unhappy.

But when Mr. Smith saw Willy he said, "How wonderful Willy is, he can walk on just his hind legs when he wants to. But when he wants to go fast he can run faster than any other dog on all four legs."

"How wonderful Willy is!" said Mrs. Smith too.

"How VERY wonderful Willy is!" shouted Harold Smith.

And Mr. Smith, Mrs. Smith and Harold Smith felt prouder of Willy than ever.

And from that day on, when Willy walked on his two hind legs, he felt happy.

When he ran on all four legs, he felt happy.

But when he just sat by the fire with Harold Smith, he felt VERY happy.

LITTLE THINGS

Julia Fletcher Carney

Little drops of water,
  Little grains of sand,
Make the mighty ocean
  And the pleasant land.

WATCH ME!

Inez Hogan

Once there was a little black bear who liked to show off.

He could roll and tumble and turn somersaults. And he would always say, "Watch ME! see what I can do."

His little sister watched him and tried to do the same things.

The mother bear watched too. One day she called her cubs to her and said, "It's about time you learned to climb a tree, come with me."

Blacky and his little sister followed Mother Bear. She led them to a tree. First she gave Blacky a boost to start him up. Blacky held on with his claws. Mother Bear gave him another boost and up he went, hugging the tree trunk.

Then Mother Bear pushed little sister. But she was afraid and began to squeal.

"Watch ME!" shouted Blacky.

"Watch ME! Watch me!
I'm climbing a TREE!"

He looked down to see if they were watching and he lost his hold and fell "Bump!" right on top of Mother Bear.

"Try again," said Mother Bear, "and this time watch what you're doing and don't try to show off."

At last both cubs learned to climb. Blacky was so pleased with himself that he stopped playing roll and tumble and spent all his time climbing.

At first he climbed only little trees, but one day Blacky looked around for the tallest tree he could find and he said to his little sister:

"Watch ME! Watch me!
I'll climb a BIG TREE."

When he was half way up Blacky stopped to rest and he shouted:

"Look at ME! Look at ME!
Half way up in the TREE."

And some one was looking at him.

It was a little gray squirrel sitting on a branch.

"What are you doing up here?" asked Blacky.

"I live in the tree," said the squirrel. "What are *you* doing up here?"

"I'm climbing," said Blacky. "Watch me, I'll show you how to climb."

"You'll show ME how to climb!" said the squirrel. "I can climb better than you can."

"I'll race you to the top of the tree."

"Let's go," said Blacky.

The squirrel leaped from branch to branch.

"I can do that," said Blacky. "Watch me!"

But there was no one to watch because the squirrel was out of sight in the top-most branches of the tree.

Blacky tried to leap like the squirrel but when he let go of the tree trunk he found himself going down instead of up. And he would have landed with a bump on the ground if he hadn't got caught in the fork of the tree.

"Ow-ow-oo," screamed the bear cub [and he pulled his nose out of the raccoon's hole] and scampered up the tree again.

This time he didn't stop climbing until he reached the top of the tree. Then he shouted:

"Look at ME!
Look at ME!
In the TOP
Of the TREE."

And a tiny little bird *was* looking at him.

"What are you doing up here?" asked Blacky.

"I live in the treetop," said the bird.

"You're so tiny," said Blacky. "What kind of a bird are you?"

"I'm a chick-a-dee," said the little bird.

"Can you climb, Chick-a-dee?" said the little black bear.

"No," said the chick-a-dee, "but I can fly."

"Well," said Blackie, "you just

"Watch ME! Watch me!
Watch me, chick-a-dee."

Blacky climbed out on the limb where the tiny bird was perched.

The chick-a-dee hopped out to the tip of the branch.

"You'd better not come out here," said the tiny bird. "You're too big, the branch will break. Now you watch what I can do."

And the tiny bird twirled 'round and 'round on a twig way out at the end of the branch.

"I can do that too," said Blacky.

"Watch ME, Chick-a-dee,
Now you watch ME."

Blacky crawled further out on the branch and tried to twirl but—the branch broke—the chick-a-

dee flew up and the little black bear went hurtling down.

Down—down—down—turning somersalts in the air—Crash! thru the branches—Crash! Bang! BUMP! on the ground.

Blacky couldn't even scream—all the wind was knocked out of him.

But Mother Bear heard the thump and came running, with little sister close behind. She nosed around her cub and licked him and rolled him over.

Little Sister began to cry.

And then Blacky's breath came back and he began to cry too.

Then Mother Bear walked away to the cave where they lived. Little sister followed and Blacky came limping along. He was a very sore little cub and he had a big bump on his head.

And after that the little black bear didn't show off so much—at least he didn't try to leap like a squirrel or do chick-a-dee tricks in the top of a tree.

BUS RIDE

Rhoda W. Bacmeister

Carl stood on the corner with his mother and looked down the sunny street to where the big, yellow bus came rolling smoothly along. It was a beautiful day for a ride and Carl danced from one foot to the other because he could hardly wait.

Now the bus was coming down his block. It rolled along importantly, making the automobiles look little beside it. Mother took Carl's hand and they went out into the street to meet it. He heard the brakes grind and the bus swerved over and stopped close beside them. Two doors popped open and folded themselves neatly back, and there were the steps and, inside, the driver waiting for them.

The steps were very high. Mother had to help Carl

up. Then she gave the driver some money, and he gave her change out of a big silver thing on his belt. "Click, click-click" it went as the money fell out into his hand.

"That must be fun," thought Carl.

They sat down close by on the first seat so Carl could watch the driver. Almost before they were ready he started the bus. "Grrrr-ah-er-wirrr" it went as he shifted the gears with a long handle that stood up beside him; then it hummed smoothly, rolling along.

"Did you pay for me this time?" Carl asked.

Mother smiled. "Not this time, Carl. See, there's the mark on the doorway right beside you that tells how tall children have to be before they pay. It's pretty high."

Just then the bus stopped to let a lady get off and Carl slipped down off the seat and stood under the mark. "Do I almost reach?" he asked.

"Well, not quite yet," said Mother. So Carl climbed back onto the seat and knelt to look out of the window. He couldn't fall out because there were little bars to keep people safe.

The big horn on the bus went "HONK-HONK" (Get out of my way, little cars!) and the bus started again with a jerk that threw Carl against Mother, so that they both laughed. Then they went down a long, straight street with lots of trees and grass and flowers, not many cars, not many houses, not many people. Just one little boy with a wagon waved to Carl.

Nobody wanted to get on.

Nobody wanted to get off.

Faster and faster they went! The wind blew hard through the open window and the whole bus bounced gently, bounce, bounce, bounce!

"Like the row boat on little waves," said Carl.

But soon the bus slowed down and went around a corner, and there Carl saw Aunt Sue and little Joe out in their yard.

"You may push the button now," Mother smiled. Carl put his thumb on the pearly button by the window and pushed it way in. That told the driver to stop, and at once the bus began to slow down, slower —slower—STOPPED!

The doors flew open and folded back, and Carl and Mother went out past the driver.

"Nice ride?" he asked Carl.

"Oh, I *liked* it," said Carl, "but by the next time I'm going to grow tall enough to pay."

"You do that," said the driver, smiling as he shut the doors and started the bus again. Then off it rolled down the street.

BILL AND HIS STEAMSHOVEL

Ruth Dennis

Once there was a man named Bill. He lived in a little green house. In the backyard he did not have any garage. He did not even have any automobile. He had a great big red steamshovel. Bill was a steamshovel man. When people wanted cellars dug, or roads made, they called up Bill, the steamshovel man.

This is what the steamshovel was like. There was a red house that had all the engines inside. Underneath there were tractor treads so that the steamshovel could go along the street. Out in front was a great big long thing like an arm. And from the end of it hung a cable. And on the end of the cable was a scoop.

But where did Bill sit when he was running the

steamshovel? He sat on a seat just inside the red house where the engines were. There he pulled the levers that made the steamshovel dig.

One morning Bill came down to breakfast and he said to his wife, "I feel like digging something today." He said, "I feel more like digging something today than I have ever felt in my life."

Bill's wife said, "Would you like to dig a cellar?"

And Bill said, "No, I am sort of tired of digging cellars."

And Bill's wife said, "Would you like to dig out a road?"

And Bill said, "No, I am sort of tired of digging roads."

"Well, what *would* you like to dig?" said Bill's wife.

"I'd like to dig a SWIMMING POOL!" said Bill.

"I like swimming pools, too," said Bill's wife. "I will put up a lunch for you . . . just in case."

So Bill's wife got out the lunch box from the cupboard next to the stove. In it she put:

Some milk in a thermos bottle
A great big ripe tomato
Three hard-boiled eggs
Four peanut-butter sandwiches and
FIVE e-*norm*ous meat sandwiches

Just as she finished putting up the lunch, the telephone rang. "Hello," said Bill. "Yes, I am Bill the steamshovel man. Yes, Mr. Jones. You'd like to have a swimming pool, Mr. Jones? I'll be right over." And he hung up.

"That was Mr. Jones," said Bill. "He wants me to dig a swimming pool. What do you know about that?"

Bill took the lunch box under his arm, kissed his wife goodbye and went out to his red steamshovel.

First he poured twenty-five gallons of gas into the tank.

Then he put oil from an oil can on different places in the engine.

Then he started up the engine.

It went rd-rd-rd-rd-rd-rd-rd-rd, something like an automobile, only much louder.

Bill climbed up inside and sat down on the little seat. He pulled one of the levers, and slowly the steamshovel began to move. Rd-rd-rd-rd-rd-rd-rd. And the tractor treads began turning. They went a little faster, and then a little faster. The steamshovel moved along the driveway, and slowly turned into the street.

Bill drove down Maple Street very, very slowly because steamshovels cannot go very fast. Also he had to be very careful to keep the scoop from getting caught in the telephone wires and the branches of trees.

Finally he came to Elm Street, where Mr. Jones lived. Mr. Jones was out in front of his house. He began waving with all his might. He said, "Right this way, Bill. Turn in here."

"Rd-rd-rd-rd-rd-rd-rd-rd . . . pf-pf-pf," went the steamshovel. Right over Mr. Jones's front lawn went the steamshovel.

"Now where shall I dig?" shouted Bill.

"Right where I have those stakes," shouted Mr. Jones.

Bill pulled the lever and the tractor treads stopped turning. The steamshovel stopped right where Mr. Jones pointed.

"Now I will begin to dig," said Bill.

Then he pulled a different lever. The scoop went up, up, up in the air until it was almost as high as Mr. Jones's house.

Then Bill let it drop, and it hit the ground with a BANG.

The motor went rd-pf-rd-pf-rd-pf-rd-pf, and it pulled up a big scoop full of dirt.

Bill touched a pedal with his foot and the whole steamshovel started turning, turning, turning. When it had turned far enough, Bill pulled a lever and CRASH, the first scoop full of dirt fell down in a pile beside the hole.

Then Bill touched the pedal on the other side, and the whole steamshovel started turning, turning, turning, back again.

Now he was ready to dig again.

Bill pulled the lever. The scoop went up, up, up in the air until finally it was just as high as Mr. Jones's house.

Then Bill let it drop and it hit the ground with a BANG.

The motor went rd-pf-rd-pf-rd-pf-rd-pf, and up came a big scoop full of dirt.

Then Bill touched the pedal with his foot, and the whole steamshovel started turning, turning, turning. When it had turned far enough, Bill pulled a lever, and CRASH, the second scoop full of dirt fell right on top of the first.

The hole was bigger and the pile of dirt was bigger.

Then Bill touched the pedal with his foot and the whole steamshovel started turning, turning, turning, back again.

If Bill could dig as fast as this, the swimming pool would be done in no time.

But then something happened.

Bill pulled the lever. The scoop went up, up, up in the air until it was *higher* than Mr. Jones's house.

Then Bill let it drop, and it hit the ground with a BANG.

But this time the motor went pf-pf-pf-pf-pf-pf-pf-pf, and the scoop did not come up at all.

Bill stopped the engine, climbed down from his seat and said, "I wonder what's the matter."

He walked around the scoop. Then he stopped and scratched his head. "I've hit a rock," he said.

"Well," he said, "I'll try again. Maybe it isn't a very *big* rock." He climbed back onto his little seat.

He started the motor again. And it went pf-pf-pf-pf-pf-pf-pf-pf. But the rock didn't move.

Bill stopped the motor. He was a little cross. He didn't like rocks.

He climbed down from his seat, walked around the scoop and scratched his head.

He looked very closely at the rock and he said, "It

is a great big rock. But I think I have moved it a little. I think I will be able to get it out next time."

He climbed back onto his little seat. He started the motor again.

This time the motor went puff! puff! puff! And suddenly the rock moved.

Then it moved some more.

The scoop rose in the air. Up, up, up.

Bill could see that the rock was TRE-*MEN*-DOUS. He was glad that he had gotten the rock out at last. It made the hole where he was digging bigger than ever.

This time he did not dump the scoop. He let it go down very, very carefully, because the rock was so big and heavy.

The rock rolled out beside the pile of dirt.

"My," said Bill, "I hope we don't have any more rocks today."

And he didn't.

He took out another scoop full of dirt.

And the hole got bigger.

He took out another scoop full of dirt.

And the hole got bigger.

He took out another scoop full of dirt.

And the hole was very, very big. And the pile of dirt beside the hole was very, very big.

Finally Bill said out loud, "Hooray, the swimming pool is finished." He stopped the engine and climbed down from the little seat. And he looked down into the hole and he said, "I think that is the best swimming pool I ever *saw*."

He took out the lunch box.

First he ate a hard-boiled egg.

Then he ate a peanut butter sandwich. That made him thirsty and he took the top off the thermos bottle. Just as he was going to drink some milk out of the thermos bottle he heard something.

He heard, "Meow, meow, meow."

What could it be?

"It must be a cat," said Bill.

He looked to the right of the steamshovel, but he didn't see it.

He looked to the left of the steamshovel, but he didn't see it.

Then he got down on his hands and knees and looked under the steamshovel.

And there was a cat, sure enough.

And there was something else, too. There were three little baby kittens lying in the grass beside their mother.

"Oh goodness," said Bill, "I am glad I didn't run over you cute little kittens with my steamshovel."

Very gently he picked up one little kitten in his hands and put him in the scoop where he would be safe.

Then he picked up another little kitten and put him in the scoop.

Then he picked up the last little kitten and put him in the scoop.

Then the mother cat jumped into the scoop next to her children.

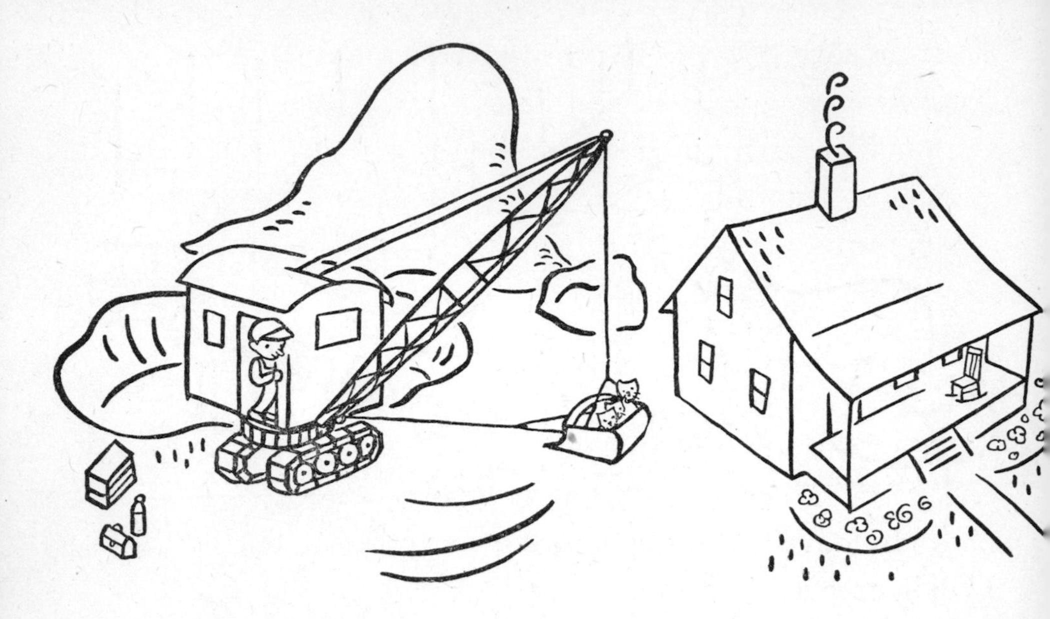

Bill climbed back on his little seat and started the motor, very, very gently. He made the motor go so slowly and so gently it hardly made any noise at all. Just rd-rd-rd-rd-rd-rd-rd-rd like a whisper.

Then he pulled the lever that made the scoop go up in the air, but very very slowly. Up, up, up in the air it went like an elevator, and the kittens were as safe as they could be.

Then Bill turned the steamshovel slowly, slowly, slowly, and let the scoop come down gently, gently, gently. The scoop came to the ground on Mr. Jones's front lawn without even a thump.

The mother cat took one of her babies in her mouth and climbed out of the scoop onto Mr. Jones's front lawn. She put the little kitten on the grass. Then she went back and got another baby kitten in her mouth and put him on the grass. Then she went back and got the third kitten in her mouth and put him on the grass. All three babies and the mother were on the grass safe and sound.

Bill said, "I think you would like the milk from my thermos bottle for your children, Mrs. Cat."

And he poured out the milk into the top of the thermos bottle. The little kittens came and drank and drank and drank. And they drank up every drop.

Just then Mr. Jones came over the lawn and said, "Mrs. Cat I'd like to know where you have been. We've been looking for you and your kittens everywhere."

Bill the steamshovel man said, "I brought them to a safe place in the steamshovel scoop. I am glad Mrs. Cat said 'meow, meow, meow' when I was eating my lunch. I might not have seen her kittens."

Bill picked up his empty thermos bottle and climbed back onto his little seat.

"Is the swimming pool all done?" asked Mr. Jones.

"Yes," said Bill. "All you have to do is get a man with a truck to take that dirt away. Then put cement around the inside of the big hole I made, and then fill it with water."

Mr. Jones smiled and smiled.

He said, "Thank you, Bill."

And Bill said, "Mr. Jones, do you know what I'd rather do than anything else in the world?"

And Mr. Jones said, "What, Bill?"

"Dig a swimming pool."

And Bill started the engine full blast. The tractor treads started turning. The steamshovel started to move, and Bill drove his big red steamshovel down the street toward his little green house.

And you could hear the engine going rd-rd-rd-rd-rd-rd-rd-rd-rd-rd-rd-rd-rd-rd-rd-rd-rd-rd-rd-rd-rd-rd-rd-rd all the way.

NEW CLOTHES

Lucy Sprague Mitchell

It was spring. It was getting warm. Bobby could feel it. It was time to put on his summer clothes. So Bobby's mother went to the closet and pulled a box down from the shelf: "Let me open it," cried Bobby. So Bobby untied the string, took off the paper and opened the box.

And what do you think he found inside? His summer sandals and all the thin clothes he had worn last summer when he had been only three years old. And now he was four. "Let's try them on," said his mother. So he tried on his thin underwear. And what do you suppose? They were so small he couldn't stand up straight when he squeezed into them. Then he tried on his sandals. And what do you suppose? They were so short he could only get his big toes in! Then he tried on his summer suits. And what do you suppose? They were so little he could hardly button

them around him. "Goody, goody!" grinned Bobby. "I'm growing so big! We'll give these clothes to little Benny, and will you get me some big ones?" "That's just exactly what I will do for my big boy," said his mother. "Where will you get them?" asked Bobby. And his mother answered, "I'll go downtown to shop."

So his mother put on her hat and coat and took her purse and started out. And where do you suppose she went? She went to a store where they kept all kinds of clothes. First she went to the counter where they had underwear. "I want to see some summer underwear for a four-year-old boy, please," she said to the girl. So the girl showed her some, but they were too small. "Bobby is bigger than that," said Bobby's mother. So the girl showed her some others, but they were too big. "Bobby's smaller than that," said Bobby's mother. So the girl showed her some others.

"These are just right, I'll take three of them, please." So the girl did up three in a package, and Bobby's mother paid her some money and took the package.

Next Bobby's mother went to the counter where they had sandals. "I want to see some summer sandals for a four-year-old boy, please," she said to the girl. So the girl showed her some white ones. "These are too light for Bobby. They'd soon get dirty," said Bobby's mother. So the girl showed her some black ones. "These are too dark for Bobby. He likes pretty colors," said Bobby's mother. So the girl showed her some colored sandals. "These are just right. I'll take one red, one blue, and one brown pair, please," said Bobby's mother. So the girl did up three pairs of sandals in a package, and Bobby's mother paid her some money and took the package.

Next Bobby's mother went to the counter where they kept summer suits. "I want to see some summer suits for a four-year-old boy, please," she said to the girl. So the girl showed her some with buttons. "These buttons are too hard for Bobby," said Bobby's mother. So the girl showed her some with straps that you wiggled into without any fastenings. "These are too easy for Bobby," said Bobby's mother. So the girl showed her some that closed with zippers. "What fun!" said Bobby's mother. "Bobby will love to zip up his suits. I'll take three—one red, one blue, and one brown, to match his sandals. But you'll have to send them—the package is too big for me to carry." So the girl did up one red, one blue and one brown suit in a package, and Bobby's mother paid her some money,

and the girl said she'd send the package that afternoon.

Now Bobby's mother had her arms full with her two packages. But she carried them both home because she knew Bobby would like it. When she got home, she gave Bobby the packages. "May I open the packages?" he asked. His mother gave him the scissors, and Bobby took the first package. He cut the string and took off the paper, and there was his new underwear. Then he took the second package. He cut the string and took off the paper, and there were his new sandals. "I like the red ones best," he said, and he smiled all over. Then he suddenly stopped smiling and looked very sad indeed. "What's the matter, Bobby boy?" asked his mother. "Don't you like your new underwear and your new sandals?" "Yes," said Bobby, "but I wanted some new suits, too!" "The suits are coming in the delivery this afternoon," said his mother. But she did not tell him what colors they were or that they had zippers.

So Bobby waited and watched and waited and watched and waited and watched, until at last up came an automobile. Out jumped a man, with a package, and ran up the steps. Bobby took the package and ran to his mother. "May I open the package?" he asked. His mother gave him the scissors. He cut the string, took off the paper, and there were his new suits—a red, a blue and a brown one; and each had a little zipper that closed and opened down the front. Bobby squealed with pleasure. "May I wear all my new things tomorrow?" cried Bobby. "Not all, my boy," laughed his mother, "but if it's warm, you may wear one set of new underwear, one pair of new sandals and one new suit!"

The next morning was warm. So Bobby put on his new underwear and it was just right. He could stand straight or bend over or jump up and down in it. Then he put on his new red sandals, for he liked them best, and they were just right. He could see his toes through the openings when he wiggled them. Then he put on his new red suit, and it was just exactly right. Zzzip! it was closed. Zzzip! it was open. Zzzip, closed. Zzzip, open. Zzzzip, zzzip, zzzip!

"Hurry up, Bobby, you'll be late for breakfast if you zip open and closed much longer," called his mother. But Bobby didn't hear a word. Zzzip! Zzzip! Zzzip!

"Where's that scallywag Bobby of mine?" called his father, coming into the room. "Oh, Daddy!" said Bobby. "Look here. Zzzip! zzzip! zzzip!" "Come along, you rascal, I'll zzzip you down stairs!" And Bobby's father tossed Bobby up to his shoulder, and they zipped downstairs and zipped into their chairs. Bobby's was higher than Daddy's or Mother's; and he could let his feet with their red sandals dangle, or he could hook them into a bar under the chair.

"I'll zip on your bib," cried Daddy, tying the bib around Bobby's neck. "Now for breakfast!" "Yes," said Bobby, "but I can still feel the zipper underneath —even if I can't see it." And while he ate his oatmeal and drank his milk, he said softly to himself, "Zzzip! Zzzip! Zzzip!"

I WENT FOR A WALK

Lois Lenski

I went for a walk
And what did I see?
The sun in the sky
Shining down on me.

Houses in yards
All along the way,
People on the sidewalk,
Happy and gay.

A woman walked by,
A man came too;
A dog wagged his tail,
A cat said mew.

Everybody smiled,
Happy as could be,
Going for a walk—
Just like me!

PEPPI AND THE CUSTARD

Rhea Wells

Peppi was a duck. Mud puddles were Peppi's chief joy in life. Whenever it rained, he would go splashing around in all the puddles he could find. It was so much fun to jump into them and see the water go flying up as his big yellow feet came plunk down on it. Peppi always went barefooted, because, if he wore shoes, he couldn't wade in the puddles.

When there had been no rain for a long time, Peppi would wait by the fountain until someone came for water. Usually some water would be spilled on the ground. Then Peppi would prance around in the puddle and pretend it was a real rain puddle. This was one of the games which he liked best.

Sometimes Peppi would take long walks in the fields outside of the walls. If he went too far, his feet would grow very tired, and then he always thought of the puddles by the fountain and wished he had one with him. He would watch the boys working in the fields and think how much nicer it was not to wear shoes. These boys wore shoes. Boys had funny feet, too, with five toes on them.

One afternoon Peppi took a very long walk. He met a little field mouse who played hide-and-seek with him in a potato field. They had such a good time that Peppi forgot to turn back until nearly dark. The shortest way home led through a dry, stubbly field. Peppi hurried along, although it hurt to step on the sharp stubble.

When he got home, his feet were terribly tired and he wanted his supper. But as he reached the kitchen door, he was much disappointed to find that the duck family had already eaten and gone to sleep.

While he stood there, hungry and thinking how his feet ached, he saw something. Sitting on the ground beside the kitchen door was a big yellow custard which the cook had put there to cool. Peppi came nearer. How nice it looked. "It must be very soft," thought Peppi. "Next to a nice mud puddle, a custard would be the finest thing in the world to rest one's feet in."

Peppi hesitated for just a second. Then he stepped into the pan. It felt so soft and comfortable. It was warm and smelled of vanilla and nutmeg. Peppi took a taste of the custard. It was very good. One taste was not enough, it was so good. He kept on eating and eating. When he was quite full, the cook came to the door to see how her custard was. She was much surprised to see a little yellow duck standing in the middle of it. "Go away, go away!" she screamed. "You are a naughty little duck and you have spoiled my custard!" the cook was very angry. "For that you get no supper!"

Peppi climbed out of the pan of custard and waddled across the courtyard. He crept under the lilac bushes and went to sleep without his supper but very full of yellow custard.

SNOW-FLAKES

Mary Mapes Dodge

Whenever a snow-flake leaves the sky,
It turns and turns to say "Good-bye!
Good-bye, dear cloud, so cool and gray!"
Then lightly travels on its way.

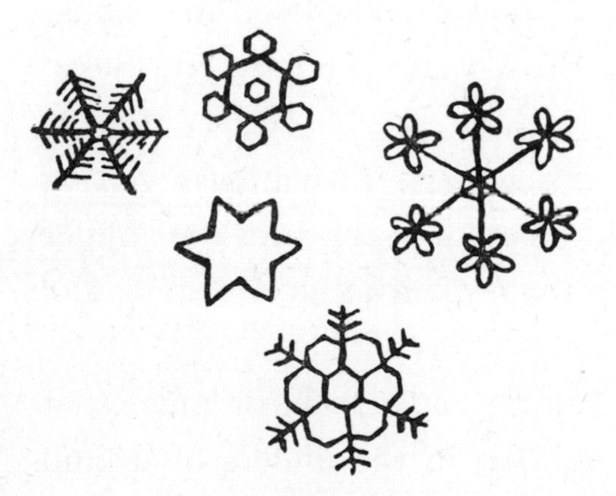

TIPPY

Inez Bertail

Tippy was a kitten. He was called Tippy because his nose and the tip of his tail were black.

Tippy lived in the country. He lived in a house with Mr. and Mrs. Brown and Tommy and Susan Brown.

Every morning, while Mrs. Brown was getting breakfast, she would give Tippy his breakfast under the kitchen sink. He always had a saucer of milk and a dish of cat food or vegetables.

After breakfast, Tippy would look for a nice spot of sunshine. He would sit in the middle of it, and clean himself. Last of all he cleaned the tip of his tail and his whiskers. Then he yawned and stretched and settled down for a little nap.

When Mr. Brown went to work, Tippy would twitch one ear or turn his head, but he went right on sleeping.

By the time Susan and Tommy were ready for school, Tippy was sitting by the front door. He would say, "Meow!" very pleasantly, and that meant, "I am ready to go out, too!"

This was a very comfortable life and Tippy was very happy with the Browns. But as he grew up, and got bigger and stronger, he sometimes felt he would like to go and live by himself.

One fine, sunny morning, Tippy decided he really was tired of living in the house—tired of milk, vegetables and cat food. He would go out and take care of himself, hunt his own food and live outdoors.

He walked down the path behind Susan and Tommy and watched while they went off to school. He looked up the road and down the road, and then decided to go off across the fields.

He walked slowly and quictly through thc tall grass. The sun was warm and the grass smelled good. He heard a faint sound ahead and saw a blade of grass move. Tippy stood very still and watched. Something jumped! It was a grasshopper. The end of Tippy's tail twitched and he pounced! But he landed too late, for the grasshopper jumped first.

Tippy pounced again, and again, but each time he was too late. So he gave up and went stalking away with the black tip of his tail waving in the air, acting as if he did not know there was a grasshopper anywhere.

Soon he came to the edge of the wood. He was hot and tired so he lay down under a shady bush and went to sleep.

He slept for quite a long time. When he woke up he was hungry. He heard birds chirping, so he sat very still and looked. He saw a little bird on a low branch. Tippy thought the bird would taste very good for dinner. He crouched and wiggled, ready to spring. But the bird saw him in time and flew up into a tree. She ruffled her feathers and smoothed them. She hopped from one branch to another, scolding Tippy so loudly and so long that he ran to get away from the noise.

It was getting late in the day and Tippy was now very hungry, and thirsty, too. He walked on to a little brook, and leaned over the edge to get a drink. Something moved in the water! Tippy's tail twitched as he saw a small fish dart away.

Tippy thought a fish would make a very good supper. He watched patiently for a long time, but no other fish swam near.

Tippy could see them farther out in the brook. So very carefully he stepped out on some stones in the water. He sat ever so still for a long, long time and finally some fish swam nearer. Tippy slowly lifted one paw. Quickly he dipped it in the brook, trying to catch the nearest fish. But the fish was too fast and darted out of sight!

Poor Tippy! He did not like having such a wet paw. He shook it, he licked it, but it was still wet.

He was still hungry, too, and he did not like being hungry. And he did not like being alone.

He thought of the Browns at home who would pet him and scratch his chin. He thought of his saucer of milk and his dish of cat food. So he hopped back on the bank and ran through the woods, across the fields, and up the path to his door.

He cried, "Meow!" "Meow!" very loudly. And that meant, "Let me in! Let me in!"

When Mrs. Brown opened the door, Tippy dashed past her into the kitchen. He looked under the sink and there was his saucer of milk. Mrs. Brown came in. He rubbed up against her legs while she gave him a dish of cat food. It tasted so good!

When he finished his supper, Tippy looked around at Mr. and Mrs. Brown and Susan and Tommy. Tommy stroked his fur and Susan scratched under his chin. Tippy stretched and yawned and curled up under Mr. Brown's chair. He blinked his eyes and purred. And that meant Tippy was happy to be home.

I'D LIKE TO BE A LIGHTHOUSE

Rachel Field

I'd like to be a lighthouse
All scrubbed and painted white.
I'd like to be a lighthouse
And stay awake all night
To keep my eye on everything
That sails my patch of sea;
I'd like to be a lighthouse
With the ships all watching me.

THE TERRRRIBLE TIGERRR

Margaret Wise Brown

Once there was a TIGER, GRRRRRRRRR, and he was four years old. Grrrrrrrrrr. And he never ate anything unless it was four years old. He ate four-year-old bugs and four-year-old chickens and four-year-old monkeys and four-year-old apples and four-year-old mice. He was a terrrrific terrrrible tigerrr. But he never ate anything that was not four years old. One day this terrible tiger met a little bit of a bug. "Little black spot of a bug," roared the terrific terrible tigerrr, "How old are you?"

"Twenty-one, twenty-two," said the little bug, "and you can't eat me, you tiger rug!"

"Grrrrrrrr," said the tiger. "Run along, little bug."

Then he lumbered along to look for his dinner,

his four-year-old dinner. Pretty soon he met a chicken hop hop hopping down the road.

"How old are you, little
Chicken chick chick?
I'm a hungrrry tigerrr,
So make it quick."

But the little chicken didn't know how old she was, so she jumped in the air and laughed like a flea. "Old tiger," she said, "I think I'm three."

"Grrrrrrrr," said the tiger, "Get away from me."

And he lumbered along to look for his dinner, his four-year-old dinner. Pretty soon he met a wild monkey.

"How old are you, little
Monkey monk monk?
I'm a hungrrry tigerrr
And could eat a hunk
Of nice and juicy
Monkey monk monk."

But the tiger was not so smart as the monk, and the monk said, "Old tiger, ask an elephant's trunk, if you really want to find out the age of this monk."

"Grrrrrrrrrr," growled the tigerrr, "I think you are junk." And he lumbered along to look for his dinner, his four-year-old dinner. "If I don't find it soon, I fear I'll grow thinner."

Pretty soon he met a mouse under an apple tree.

"Mouse, mouse, under the tree,
Are you old enough
To be dinner for me?"

"No," squeaked the mouse, "I'm only three, and so are the apples on this tree."

"Then I won't eat you.
Get away from me."
And the tiger bit
At the bark of the tree.
"I'm terrrribly hungry—
But you're only three."

The little mouse squeaked, "That's a nice age to be." And the terrrrible tigerrr lumbered along to look for his dinner, his four-year-old-dinner. He lumbered along and he lumbered along and he lumbered along and he lumbered along. And he sang a tiger's hungry song.

"I'm a hungrrry tigerrr,
I am, I am,
With nothing to eat
But strawberry jam—"

So he lumbered along and he lumbered along until he was even too hungry to sing a song. There just didn't seem to be anything that day that was four years old to eat. But pretty soon he came to a street that had all sorts of wonderful things to eat, and all of a sudden he roared, "I SMELL MEAT! Four-year-old meat, and it is hiding some place on this street. Meat, MEAT, meat for to eat!" And he rushed and he roared and he lumbered down the street, a terrrrible tigerrr looking for meat. He looked in the grocer's, but it wasn't there. Only the grocer combing his hair. He looked in a fruit store, but it wasn't there. Only the storekeeper eating a pear. He looked in a candy store, hungry as a bear. He looked in a taxi, he looked everywhere; he even looked under a policeman's chair. But it wasn't there. It wasn't anywhere. He was ready to stop. And then he came to a butcher shop.

"Old butcher," he said,
"I smell meat.
Please, old butcher,
Give me something to eat—
Something delicious
Like FOUR-YEAR-OLD MEAT."

The butcher sniffed,

"Old terrible tiger,
I've fresh roast beef
And fresh lamb chops;
I've liver and pork
And pink lollypops;
I even have some
Old blue meat
That is four years old
And the people won't eat.
And four years old is
A *long* time for meat."

But the tiger roared, "This *will* be a treat," and he filled up his tummy with four-year-old meat. He ate all he could hold, then he rolled down the street. But he didn't really like four-year-old meat. Four-year-old meat is too old to eat.

He met a small boy at the end of the street who

GROCERY
FRUIT
MEAT
LOIS
LENSKI

was trying to count all the toes on his feet.

"How old are you,
Little very small boy?
I'm not very hungry,
But still I enjoy
A bit of fun
With a four-year-old boy."

The little boy looked up from counting his toes.

"Old tiger," he said,
"By the twitch of your nose,
I am five years old,
As everyone knows."

"Oh dear," said the tiger, "I've eaten and I'm through. I don't like old meat that is cold and blue. I like ZEBRAS and RABBITS and WILD KANGAROO, that are delicious and tender and four years old, too."

And the little boy said, "There's not much on this street but butchers and grocers and stale things to eat. Why don't you go back to the Jungles and heat, where the bushes are teeming with four-year-old meat?"

"Grrrrrrrrrr," growled the tigerrr,
"I guess you are right."
And he galloped away,
Far away out of sight.

WHY DO THE BELLS OF CHRISTMAS RING?

Eugene Field

Why do the bells of Christmas ring?
Why do little children sing?

Once a lovely shining star,
Seen by shepherds from afar,
Gently moved until its light
Made a manger's cradle bright.

There a darling baby lay
Pillowed soft upon the hay;
And its mother sang and smiled:
"This is Christ, the holy Child!"

Therefore bells for Christmas ring,
Therefore little children sing.

WEE ROBIN'S CHRISTMAS DAY

There was once an old gray pussy-cat, and she went down by the waterside, and there she saw Wee Robin Redbreast, hopping on a brier.

And Pussy-Cat said, "Where are you going, Wee Robin?"

And Wee Robin said, "I am going away to the king, to sing him a song this good Christmas morning."

And Pussy-Cat said, "Come here, Wee Robin, and I will let you see the bonny white ring around my neck."

But Wee Robin said: "No, no, Gray Pussy; no, no. You worried the wee mousie, but you shall not worry me."

So Wee Robin flew away and away, until he came to a turf wall, and there he saw a gray greedy hawk.

And the gray greedy hawk said, "Where are you going, Wee Robin?"

And Wee Robin said, "I am going away to the

king, to sing him a song this good Christmas morning."

And the gray greedy hawk said, "Come here, Wee Robin, and I will let you see the bonny white feather in my wing."

But Wee Robin said: "No, no, Gray Greedy Hawk; no, no. You pecked at the wee linnet, but you shall not peck me."

So Wee Robin flew away until he came to the side of a rock, and there he saw a sly fox sitting.

And the sly fox said, "Where are you going, Wee Robin?"

And Wee Robin said, "I am going away to the king to sing him a song this good Christmas morning."

And the sly fox said, "Come here, Wee Robin, and I will let you see the bonny white spot on the tip of my tail."

But Wee Robin said: "No, no, Sly Fox; no, no. You worried the wee lamb, but you shall not worry me."

Wee Robin flew away until he came to a bonny wood, and there he saw a wee boy sitting, and the wee boy said, "Where are you going, Wee Robin?"

And the Wee Robin said, "I am going away to the king, to sing him a song this good Christmas morning."

And the wee boy said, "Come here, Wee Robin, and I will give you some nice crumbs out of my pocket."

But Wee Robin said: "No, no, Wee Boy; no, no. You threw stones at the chickadee, but you shall not throw stones at me."

So Wee Robin flew away and away, until he came to the king, and there he sat on a widow sill and sang to the king a bonny song.

And the king said to the queen, "What shall we give to Wee Robin for singing us this bonny song?"

And the queen said to the king, "I think we will give him the wee wren for his wife."

So Wee Robin and the wee wren were married, and all the court danced at the wedding.

CHILD AT A WINDOW

Janette Sebring Lowrey

I

I thought it was a leaf,
It came so gently to rest,
But it wasn't a leaf,
It was little yellow-breast.

He came into my tree
With scarce a flutter of his wings,
And now, not far from me,
He sits and sweetly sings.

II

Open your window.
What do you see?

A robin, two sparrows,
  Wrens, one, two, and three,
A lizard, a spider,
  A wasp, and a bee,
Clouds in the heavens,
  Leaves on the tree.

Open your window.
  What do you hear?

Wind in the treetops,
  A brook splashing near,
A bell in a steeple
  That rings loud and clear,
And a little bird singing,
  "What cheer?" and "What cheer?"

Open your window
  What will come in?

Rose-petal perfume,
  Smoke, blue and thin,
The sparkle of sunshine,
  A breath of cool wind,
And a thistledown top
  That a fairy might spin.

MICHAEL THE COLT

Katharine T. Garbutt

When Michael was just three minutes old, he lay on the straw in a shed, but he didn't like lying there. He wanted to stand up. All good baby colts want to stand up right away, and Michael was a good baby colt!

So Michael tried to get up. He tried first with his front legs. And then with his hind legs.

It was hard because his legs kept getting mixed up and thcy were so long they wobbled a great deal. But, at last, there he was standing up on all four legs for the first time.

Then he tried to walk—first one foot and then the other, very carefully so that he wouldn't fall down. Ahead of him was the open door of his shed. He walked toward it very slowly.

At last he was outside!

And there, out in the bright sun and the green

grass, he found his mother, who had been watching him all this time. His mother's name was Queen. She nudged him with her soft warm nose and he was happy.

All that day, Michael learned things. He learned to lie under his mother in the shade.

He learned where his mother's nice bag of milk was. He drank some whenever he wanted.

He didn't have to switch his tail to keep the flies away because his tail seemed to know that all by itself, and kept switching back and forth, back and forth, every minute. But Michael did learn to stand under his mother's tail and let her brush some of the flies off for him.

Then he tried to learn to stamp the way his mother did, but that was hard. He kept getting his front legs crossed when he tried, and then he couldn't seem to get them uncrossed again.

His neck itched and he tried to scratch it with one hind foot but that was terribly hard to do. Then he tried it with the other hind foot and that was just as hard. He almost sat down he tried so hard.

Michael discovered that the best way to learn how to do things was to watch his mother. He watched his mother eating grass and thought it would be fun for him to eat grass, too. So he stretched his neck down as far as it would go, but he couldn't reach the ground. His legs were too long. Then he spread his front legs wide apart and tried again. That worked, and he took a nibble of grass, but it didn't taste half as nice as his mother's warm milk. He didn't know that horses have to grow up before they like to eat grass.

When Michael was a week old, he had begun to walk straight and steady beside his mother. Then he tried to run a step or two. Sometimes he went off a little way by himself but he was always glad to have his mother answer when he called. He felt safe when he knew she was near by.

The field where Michael and his mother lived seemed large to Michael but it was really quite small. It had a wooden fence around it and a shed at one end. It was in the middle of a big city.

Every day horses went by outside the fence. There were all sorts of horses and all sorts of riders, because the City Park where people rode horseback was very near.

Michael loved to watch the horses go by. His mother just went on eating grass, but Michael was excited. He watched for them every day.

And when they came, Michael raced back and forth by the fence. He held his tail high in the air and tried to look like the grown-up horses outside.

Now Michael was about two weeks old, and he

wanted to play. But he couldn't find anyone to play with him. He tried to play with his mother but that didn't do. One day he played too hard and she bit him just enough to tell him to be good. Michael was so surprised that he was cross. He put back his ears and whirled around, and then he was very naughty. He tried to kick! He tried so hard he almost tumbled over, but his mother didn't even notice. So that wasn't any fun.

"Steady!" and "Whoa, there!" said the man who came to feed Michael's mother. He didn't understand that Michael wanted to play with him. Michael tried all sorts of games. He even tried kicking and then he stood on his hind legs and hit out with his front legs.

When he did that he almost fell down again. The man laughed and laughed. Michael didn't want the man to laugh, he wanted him to play, so the next time the man brought a bucket of grain for Queen, Michael gave him a little bite, just the way his mother had bitten him to make him be good. But the man only said, "Ouch!" The man wasn't any fun.

"Cock-a-doodle-do! Cock-a-doodle-do!"

When Michael heard the rooster he ran to play with him. But the rooster was busy looking for a worm. He didn't want to play either!

"Bow-wow! Bow-wow!" said the dog. But when Michael asked him to play, the dog ran away.

He said he had to get an important bone he had hidden.

"Meow! Meow! Meow!" The cat came close to Michael. Se seemed very friendly. She purred and purred. But, all of a sudden, she saw a mouse in the long grass, and away she went to catch it. So Michael couldn't play with the cat.

Poor Michael. He couldn't find anyone to play with. He was very sad.

Now the man who didn't have time to play was watching Michael every day and he knew that Michael was unhappy. He saw that Michael didn't have much room to play and no one to play with. He decided to give Queen and Michael a surprise.

One day when Michael was four weeks old a big box on wheels came to the fence. The man let down the bars and Queen walked in. Michael was frightened at first, but he walked in beside his mother. Inside there was nice hay and, when Queen began to eat it, Michael felt better. It was almost like being in his shed.

Then the box began to move, but Michael didn't mind because his mother didn't mind. The man had called the box a trailer and Michael decided that he liked trailers. He was having an adventure!

He stood up straight beside his mother. He looked over the edge. He looked at his mother. When the roads were rough he bumped against his mother. She felt warm and comfortable. Michael was excited and he wasn't sad any more.

All at once they stopped with a jerk. The man got out and opened the door to their trailer. Queen backed out but Michael turned around and slid down. Michael wondered where they were.

Then the man led Queen and Michael up a hill. The grass was so long it tickled Michael's stomach. They climbed up and up and at the top they stopped. Michael looked and looked.

Over the top of the hill was a field. It was a very big field with trees and a river and lots and lots of long grass. But – most important of all – were the horses–all kinds–big ones like Queen and colts like Michael–hundreds of them, Michael thought. When they saw Michael, they stopped eating. One of the colts hurried over to meet him. At first, Michael thought he would like to hide behind his mother and then he remembered that he was four weeks old, and he wasn't afraid.

When the new colt came near, all at once, Michael knew that he wanted to P L A Y ! Michael kicked up his heels and ran with his new friend to join the others. And all day, every day, Michael played. He played in the rain. He played in the warm sun.

And he was very happy.

I'M GLAD

I'm glad the sky is painted blue,
   And the earth is painted green,
With such a lot of nice fresh air
   All sandwiched in between.

SEEING THE WORLD

Marion Florence Lansing

A little pig was standing at the door of his sty. His mother stood behind him.

"Ho, ho!" said the little pig, "the farmer boy has left this door ajar and I can push it open. I have always wanted to see the world, and now is my time. I'm off."

"No, no," said his mother; "stay here with me. You will be safer in the sty."

"No," said the little pig; "I have always wanted to see the world, and I'm going. It would be of no use for you to come. You would be in my way, and in your own as well, for I know you do not care to see the world. Good-by."

"Take care, take care. It may be well to go out in the world if you must, but it is best to stop at home if you can," called his mother.

"Poor old thing!" said the little Pig, and out he walked into the farmyard. It had a low stone wall around it.

"So this is the world," thought the little pig. "What a large place it is. Dear me, I must take care or I shall be lost. I must keep close to the edge of the world. Then I shall not lose my way."

"Quack, quack," called two geese, standing in his way and putting out their heads at him.

"I don't like this," said little pig. "I'll go as fast as I can."

"Cluck, cluck, cluck, cluck," cried four hens that were standing by the wall a little farther on.

"What does this mean? How much I shall have to tell when I get home!" On he went until he came to a door. A red cow was standing there.

"This must be the end of the world. See that great, ugly pig with the big horns. I will get out of her way as fast as I can. I will make haste. Why, here I am back at the door of my own sty."

"So here you are back again," said his mother, when she saw him.

"Here I am."

"What have you seen?" she asked.

"Oh, such things. I have been round the world. I find it is square and has a wall all around it, lest pigs should fall off. In fact it is like a big sty."

"Well, to be sure!" said his mother.

"And the end of the world is made of wood and has two high posts, one on each side to mark the place. The first thing that I saw in the world was a pair of the queerest pigs. They had but two legs, and they had very long necks. There are but two in the world. Think of that! Then I saw four smaller pigs, and they said 'Cluck, cluck, cluck, cluck.'"

"What does that mean?" asked his mother.

"Oh, it is what they say in the world. It is of no use to tell you what it means, for you have not been there, and you wouldn't understand. Then I saw a huge red pig with two horns. There is but one pig of this sort in the whole world."

"Well, to be sure!" said his mother.

"I should have made friends with her, but she did not look my way. And then as I had gone all round the world, I came home. Ah, the world is a fine place. To think that you have never seen it, you poor old thing. Now the farmer boy may shut the door when he likes. I know all about the world."

"Well, to be sure!" said his mother as she trotted off.

THE DUCK UMBRELLA

Lois Lenski

Pitter, patter on the roof. It was Sunday afternoon and it was raining hard. Mr. and Mrs. Beanstalk sat reading by the table. A car honked its horn outside. Benny ran to the window to see.

"It's Uncle Ben! It's Uncle Ben!" he called. He ran out to meet him on the porch.

Uncle Ben was the finest Uncle in the world. He had a bald head. He knew all about boats and fish-worms and wasps. When he came in he was carrying a large umbrella. It was dripping wet. Benny took it and put it in the rack. Uncle Ben's coat pocket was very fat. Benny put in his hand and took out a bag of marbles. He put in his hand again and took out a box of crayons. Uncle Ben knew how to play marbles and how to draw boats. He knew why fishworms squirm and why wasps sting.

Soon it was time for supper. Then it was time for Uncle Ben to go.

Benny said, "Why can't you stay always?"

Uncle Ben shook his head.

Father and Mother and Benny waved goodbye from the porch. Then they came indoors.

"Look!" cried Mother. "There is Uncle Ben's umbrella!" There it was in the rack. Yes, Uncle Ben forgot his umbrella. He usually forgot something, sometimes a handkerchief or a shirt. This time it was his umbrella.

The next morning a letter came from Uncle Ben. It said: "Dear Benny:

> I left Mr. Duck behind. Please take good care of him. Don't let him walk away! I will get him the next time I come.
>
> With love,
>
> Uncle Ben."

Benny took the umbrella out of the rack and looked at it. It was a fine umbrella, a most unusual umbrella. It had a Duck handle. The head was white ivory with black bead eyes. The bill was black ebony. It was a fine Duck who looked as if he could almost quack. When the umbrella was open, it was very large. Larger than Father's old brown one or Mother's blue silk one or Sister's torn red one. Benny opened and closed it many times. It never pinched his fingers.

Uncle Ben was the finest Uncle in the world. So Uncle Ben's Duck Umbrella was the finest umbrella in the world. And that's why Benny took such good care of it—or tried to.

* * *

The next morning, Benny jumped up and ran to the window. He rubbed his nose on the glass. The rain was running down the glass in little rivers on the outside.

"Today I can take Mr. Duck," he said to himself.

Father took his old brown umbrella to go to the store. Mother took her best silk one when she went out to feed the chickens. Sister ran off with her torn red one.

Benny opened the Duck umbrella on the porch. How nice and smooth and shiny the duck's head

was. He tipped the umbrella back over his shoulder. He held his book and lunch box in the other hand.

Benny walked slowly. He stopped. He splashed in a mud puddle. He kicked a stone and watched it roll into the puddle. He found a stick and sailed it in the ditch. The rain stopped and the sun came out. He put his book and lunch box down. He closed the umbrella and laid it down in the grass. The boat sailed faster and faster down the little stream. Benny thought what fun it must be to sail in a boat all day long. All day long over beautiful rivers and ponds and lakes.

The sun came out and warmed the air. A bird sang cheerily in a near-by bush. A bell rang in the distance.

At first Benny did not hear it. It rang the second time. And then Benny heard. He picked up his book and his lunch box and ran. But he never thought of Mr. Duck lying hidden in the grass.

Poor Mr. Duck! He could not call, "Quack! Quack!"

In the afternoon on the way home, Benny remembered. He looked for the umbrella everywhere, but it was gone. Father looked for it, too, and so did Sister and Mother. No one could find it.

Benny was very unhappy until Mother said, "Never mind! Just wait! It'll turn up one of these days. Umbrellas always do!"

They all laughed.

So Benny waited for it to turn up. Little did he guess that Mr. Duck would travel far and wide before he came home again.

* * *

On the same morning that Benny lost the umbrella, Miss Sally Pippin woke up early. She rubbed her glasses clean and looked out. The rain made her think of spring. Spring made her wish for a new hat. Or a new flower for her old hat.

After breakfast Miss Sally put on her old hat. She looked in the mirror and shook her head. Then she took her umbrella and started down the street. She had not gone far when the sun came out. She put down her umbrella. She stopped by a bush to hear a bird singing. There in front of her, in the grass, lay another umbrella, a large one. Miss Sally picked it up.

"A very unusual umbrella," said Miss Sally. "'Tisn't every umbrella has a duck's head for a handle! Now who could have lost it?"

Miss Sally looked very funny carrying two umbrellas, one under each arm. She walked briskly and hummed a little tune. The birds chirped and sang over her head.

Soon she reached the store. It was Mrs. Pickle's Store. Mrs. Pickle had a very sour face, just like her name. On rainy days she was cross. On sunny days she was cross. She was very, very cross when Miss Sally Pippin came in.

Miss Sally forgot all about a new spring hat. She forgot all about a new flower for her old hat. She was thinking of the lost umbrella. She wanted to find the owner. It must belong to somebody. She could not think who. Farmer Turnip? No. Mrs. Pancake? Hardly. Joe Doorstep? Never.

"Do you think it belongs to Dr. Teaspoon?" She held it out in front of her.

But Mrs. Pickle would not even look. She put her head in the cracker barrel and said, "Don't know and don't care!"

"Very well," said Miss Sally Pippin.

PICKLE
STORE
LOIS
LENSKI

Up went her chin. Down went her lips. With one umbrella under each arm she walked out. At the door she turned and said,

"I *was* going to buy a new hat, but I've changed my mind." Miss Sally Pippin's cheeks were red. Her eyes were bright. "I will find the owner of the Duck Umbrella myself." She walked down the street.

* * *

She had not gone very far before she met old Mr. Bones. Old Mr. Bones liked to walk to town every day. He liked to go to the postoffice to ask for the mail. There never were any letters for him, but he did not care. It was a nice walk home again. He was a little deaf, but still he could hear the birds singing. It sounded as if they were far away, but he liked it.

Miss Sally Pippin said, "Good morning."

Old Mr. Bones, who never forgot his manners, took off his hat and bowed. He smiled sweetly and

began to talk. Then he saw something funny. Miss Sally was carrying two umbrellas. He looked and looked at the umbrellas and started to say something.

Miss Sally did not hear what he was saying. Miss Sally began to talk about umbrellas. She began to wave them about. She began to ask questions about umbrellas. Old Mr. Bones kept on saying, "Yes, yes." Then she put the large umbrella with the Duck handle into his hands. Old Mr. Bones, who was always polite, said, "Thank you." He turned and watched her. She walked quickly up the street and went home.

Old Mr. Bones had wanted an umbrella for a long time. He was glad to get one. Now he could walk in the rain. He would not get his clothes wet. He would not take cold and have to stay in bed. And a nice duck for company—why, it looked as if it could almost quack! How kind of Miss Sally to give it to him. He did not go to the post office after all. There never were any letters anyhow. He forgot about mail and started for home. He opened and shut his new umbrella many times on the way home.

* * *

He walked slowly. He felt a little tired so he sat down on the side of the road to rest. Just then a load of hay came along. Farmer Cabbagehead called out, "Want a ride?"

Old Mr. Bones climbed up on top of the hay. He threw the umbrella down beside him. He talked to the farmer about many things. When they came to his house, he climbed down. He left the umbrella on top, but he did not know it. Poor Mr. Duck! He could not call, "Quack! Quack!"

* * *

Farmer Cabbagehead drove into the lane with the load of hay. He called loudly to his son Johnny. Johnny came and helped pitch the hay into the mow. They worked a long time. They did not know that they pitched an umbrella into their haymow. No one knew it, no one but a mouse who made her nest in the folds of the umbrella that night. It made a good bed for her babies.

But Mrs. Mouse was not good at keeping secrets. That night she told the pig. The pig told the calf. The calf told the cow. The cow told the old gray horse. So the whole barn knew that a funny duck who could not quack lay hidden in the hay. Only the ducks were cross about it. The other animals thought it very funny and made a great deal of noise. All the hens began to cackle.

Farmer Cabbagehead woke up. He put his head out of the window. The moon was shining. He called out, "Who's there?" No one answered, so he went back to bed. By and by the animals and chickens went to sleep too. Mrs. Mouse and her babies had pleasant dreams in their soft umbrella nest.

Days passed. The animals remembered the Duck umbrella all summer. Every time Johnny threw down hay they watched, to see if it would come down. One day it *did* come down, but they were all out in the pasture. So they never saw it.

Poor Mr. Duck! He could not call "Quack!

Quack!" To this day they still talk about the umbrella in the haymow.

* * *

Johnny threw down an armful of hay. He jumped down on top of it. He jumped on something hard. He looked. He picked it up.

"Why, hello, Mr. Duck," thought Johnny. "What a nice umbrella. But how did it ever get up there?" He took it in the house, to show to his mother. She was busy making cookies and did not want to be bothered. She said, "That old thing! Take it up to the attic!"

Johnny took it up to the attic. He put it in a trunk. He sprinkled moth balls all over it.

"It's not old, at all," he said to himself. "It's a good umbrella, and I do like that duck's head."

The lid of the trunk came down with a bang. Poor Mr. Duck! He could not call, "Quack! Quack!"

* * *

Days passed and autumn came. One morning it was very windy and blowy. All the gay red leaves were falling from the trees. Little Susie Cabbagehead, who was six, had a bad cold. Her mother put her to bed on the sofa. Then she went to the attic to get some flannel. There on the top lay a fine umbrella with a duck's head for a handle.

Mrs. Cabbagehead brushed it off carefully. She was sure she had never seen a Duck Umbrella before. How did it get into the trunk? It must belong to somebody. She took it downstairs and put it in the rack.

She wrapped the flannel around Susie's throat. In a few minutes a car stopped in front of the house and someone knocked at the door. It was Dr. Teaspoon.

He carried a small black bag. He made Susie put out her tongue. On the table he put some pills and powders for her to take, after meals and at bedtime. He

talked awhile with Mrs. Cabbagehead. Then he put on his coat and hat and picked up an umbrella from the rack. It was raining hard, so he put it up and walked out to his car.

When he reached his office he found Mr. Duck in his hand.

"Why, where did I get this umbrella? Somebody must have given it to me. What a funny duck handle it has! It looks just as if it could quack!"

He put it in the umbrella rack in his office, just inside the door. The very next patient who came to call, picked it up and carried it away with him. It happened to be Mr. Grapefruit.

When Mr. Grapefruit was half way home, he stopped and leaned the umbrella against a large tree. He put his hand up to his head, because it was aching badly. "I forgot to stop at the drug store to get that medicine," he said. "I must go back."

He left the umbrella leaning against the tree.

Poor Mr. Duck! He could not call "Quack! Quack!"

There Jimmy Freckles found it. "Whew!" he whistled. "A duck's head!"

He opened the umbrella up. "As big as a parachute!" He whistled again.

LOIS
LENSKI

The tree had a large, strong branch leaning out over the sidewalk. Jimmy tucked the umbrella under his arm and began to climb up.

"Quack, quack!" he kept saying out loud.

When he got out on the branch, he opened the umbrella again. He stood up and walked along the branch, using it to balance with. But the branch was pretty high from the ground. Jimmy did not jump.

"Quack, quack!" he kept saying.

* * *

It was Sunday again, but this time the sun was shining. Mr. and Mrs. Beanstalk sat reading by the table. A car honked its horn outside.

"Uncle Ben! It's Uncle Ben!" called Benny. He ran to meet him.

Benny remembered the lost umbrella. Every day he had looked in the rack for it, but it had not turned up as Mother said.

Benny opened the door. But he did not look for fat pockets this time. He did not jump into Uncle Ben's arms. He did not say "Hello." He just stared in surprise.

For there in Uncle Ben's hand was the Duck Umbrella!

"Wh—wh—where did you find it, Uncle Ben?"

Uncle Ben laughed. "It dropped from the sky!"

"Oh *no*, Uncle Ben. It couldn't do that!" said Benny.

"Ducks like to swim and umbrellas like to travel," said Uncle Ben. "But *my* Mr. Duck took it into his head to fly!"

"To fly?" said Benny.

Supper was ready and they sat down to eat. Then Uncle Ben explained:

"I pulled up at a red light down the street, right beside a big tree. I heard a noise—quack, quack! I saw something that looked like a big, black cloud . . ."

"What was it, Uncle Ben?"

"Down from the sky came a big umbrella floating!

It was wide open. I reached out and caught it by the handle, and it was . . ."

"Mr. Duck!" added Benny. "But how . . . but who . . ."

"A boy called Jimmy was up in the tree, playing parachute. The branch was so high he was afraid to jump, so he let go of the handle, and there he was hanging onto that branch with all his might, while Mr. Duck flew down through the air right into my hand!"

They all laughed.

"Where do you suppose Jimmy found it?" asked Benny. "It's been gone all summer long."

"He said he found it leaning against the tree," said Uncle Ben. "Perhaps Mr. Duck took a walk down the street. Then he got tired and stopped for a rest!"

"Looks like he's been traveling all summer," said Benny.

When it was time to go, Benny followed Uncle Ben to the door and said, "Don't forget your umbrella, Uncle Ben!"

Uncle Ben picked it up and said, "Well, Mr. Duck, old fellow, if you could only talk, you could tell us where you've been, couldn't you?"

But Mr. Duck did not answer.

Poor Mr. Duck! He could not say "Quack! Quack!"

THE STAR

Jane Taylor

Twinkle, twinkle, little star,
How I wonder what you are,
Up above the world so high,
Like a diamond in the sky.

When the blazing sun is set,
And the grass with dew is wet,
Then you show your little light,
Twinkle, twinkle, all the night.

Then the traveler in the dark
Thanks you for your tiny spark,
He could not see where to go
If you did not twinkle so.

In the dark blue sky you keep,
And often through my curtains peep,
For you never shut your eye
Till the sun is in the sky.

As your bright and tiny spark
Lights the traveler in the dark,
Though I know not what you are,
Twinkle, twinkle, little star.

SUSIE'S SLEEPY TIME

Corinna Marsh

It was Susie's bedtime. But Susie didn't want to go to sleep. Too many nice things were happening.

The sun was red but not yet in bed. The winds were sighing and the birds were flying, and the little boy next door was crying.

Susie wanted to know what was going to happen next. She didn't want to go to sleep.

Susie's toys were all put away in the toy box, and her doll was already fast asleep in her little doll cradle. Susie had been to the bathroom and brushed her teeth and had a drink of water.

She had on her blue pajamas and her blue-and-white bathrobe and her slippers with the funny little white bunny faces on them.

She had given Daddy a big hug and a good-night kiss and Mummy had come into her room to tuck her into bed.

Mummy kissed her good night and said, "See, Susie, the sun is getting red; he's ready to go to bed. Slower and slower and slower he's sinking lower and lower and lower, and soon he will be asleep."

The winds had stopped sighing and the birds had stopped flying and the little boy next door had stopped crying. And all the mothers in the world were saying 'HUSHshshshshshshshshsh!"

Then Mummy pulled down the window shades and Susie's room was all nice and sleepy-cool and sleepy-dark and sleepy-still.

But still Susie didn't want to go to sleep.

She could hear Tom coming down the road with the cows.

"MOO," mooed the cows as they went by. "MOO-ooooooooooooooo" they mooed slower and slower and lower and lower till Susie couldn't hear them any more at all.

The evening mail plane came flying by.

Grrrrrrrrrrr," grrrrd the plane as it flew over the house. "Grrrrrrrrrrrrrr" it grrrd, slower and slower and lower and lower and lower till Susie couldn't hear it any more at all.

A long, long, long freight train came chugging by. It came from far, far, far away. "CHUCK-A-CHOO, CHUCK-A-CHOO, CHUCK-A-CHOO," it chugged as it went past the station. Then it went far, far, far away down into the valley. "CHUCK-A-CHOO, CHUCK-a-chooooooooooo," it chugged slower and slower and lower and lower till Susie couldn't hear it any more at all.

The birds in the tree outside Susie's window were saying good night to each other. "CHIRP-CHIRP, TWEET-TWEET, TWITTER-TWITTER," they said, meaning, in bird language, "Good-night, Pleasant dreams, Sleep tight." But soon they were saying "Chirp-chirp, Tweet-tweet, Twitter-twitter," slower and slower and lower and lower until Susie couldn't hear them any more at all because they were all fast asleep.

"HUSHshshshshshshshsh," whispered the leaves in the trees, "HUSHshshshshshshshsh."

Susie's eyelids were beginning to be very, very heavy. They were dropping lower and lower and lower and slowly closing, closing, closing.

Mummy was singing, "Sleep, Susie, sleep—sleep, Susie, sleep" slower and slower and lower and lower till Susie couldn't hear her any more at all—because Susie was asleep.

A CHILD'S GRACE

Mrs. E. R. Leatham

Thank you for the world so sweet,
Thank you for the food we eat,
Thank you for the birds that sing,
Thank you, God, for everything.